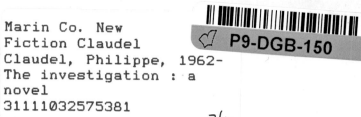

P9-DGB-150

DATE DUE

THE INVESTIGATION

ALSO BY PHILIPPE CLAUDEL

PUBLISHED IN ENGLISH

Brodeck

By a Slow River

THE INVESTIGATION

A NOVEL

PHILIPPE CLAUDEL

TRANSLATED FROM THE FRENCH BY JOHN CULLEN

NAN A. TALESE | DOUBLEDAY
NEW YORK LONDON TORONTO SYDNEY AUCKLAND

NAN A. TALESE | DOUBLEDAY

www.nanatalese.com

Originally published in France as *L'Enquête* by Éditions Stock, Paris, in 2010. Copyright © 2010 by Éditions Stock. This edition published by arrangement with Éditions Stock.

Book design by Pei Loi Koay
Jacket design and illustration by Emily Mahon

LIBRARY OF CONGRESS CATALOGING-IN-PUBLICATION DATA
Claudel, Philippe
[Enquête. English]
The investigation : a novel / Philippe Claudel ; translated from the French by John Cullen.—1st U.S. ed.
p. cm.
"Originally published in France as L'Enquête by Éditions Stock, Paris, in 2010."
I. Cullen, John. II. Title.
PQ2663.L31148E5713 2012
843'.914—dc23
2011034662

ISBN 978-0-385-53534-2

MANUFACTURED IN THE UNITED STATES OF AMERICA

10 9 8 7 6 5 4 3 2 1

First American Edition

For those to come

so they won't be next

Seek nothing. Forget.

—HENRI-GEORGES CLOUZOT, *L'Enfer*

THE INVESTIGATION

W HEN THE INVESTIGATOR LEFT the train station, a fine rain mingled with melting snow greeted him. He was a small, slightly round fellow with thinning hair, and nothing about him, neither his clothes nor his expression, was remarkable. Anyone obliged to describe him—as part of a novel, for example, or in a criminal proceeding or judiciary testimony—would surely have found it difficult to give a detailed portrait of the man. The Investigator was, in a way, a disappearing person, no sooner seen than forgotten. His aspect was as insubstantial as fog, dreams, or an expelled breath, and in this he resembled billions of human beings.

The station square resembled countless other station squares, surrounded by impersonal buildings crowded against one another. Across the top of one of these tall structures, a giant billboard displayed the hugely enlarged photograph of an old man, who gazed down at the viewer with amused, melancholy eyes. The slogan accompanying the picture was illegible and maybe even nonexistent; the Investigator couldn't tell, because the upper part of the billboard was hidden in clouds.

The sky was crumbling and falling in a wet dust that dissolved on shoulders and then, uninvited, entered every body part. It wasn't really cold, but the dampness acted like an octopus whose slender tentacles managed to find their way into the tiniest open spaces between skin and clothing.

For a quarter of an hour, the Investigator kept still, standing upright with his suitcase on the pavement beside him, while raindrops and snowflakes continued to expire on his head and raincoat. He didn't move, not at all. And during that long moment, he thought about nothing.

No vehicle passed. No pedestrian. He'd been forgotten. It wasn't the first time. Eventually, he turned up the collar of his raincoat, grasped the handle of his suitcase, and resolved to walk across the square to a bar before he got completely drenched. The lights in the bar were already on, even though the clock mounted on a lamppost a few yards away from him indicated that it wasn't yet four in the afternoon.

The room was curiously empty, and the Waiter, who'd been dozing behind the bar while distractedly watching the horse-racing results on a television screen, cast a less-than-friendly glance in the Investigator's direction. He had time enough to remove his raincoat, take a seat at a table, and wait a little before the Waiter asked in a doleful voice, "What would you like?"

The Investigator was neither very thirsty nor very hungry. He simply needed to sit down someplace before betaking himself to where he was supposed to go. He needed to sit down, to assess the situation, to prepare what he was going to say, and little by little to enter, as it were, into his persona as the Investigator. Finally, he said, "A rum toddy."

The Waiter quickly answered, "I'm sorry, but that's impossible."

"You don't know how to make a rum toddy?" asked the Investigator in surprise.

The Waiter shrugged his shoulders. "Of course I do, but that particular beverage isn't included in our computerized list, and the automated cash register will refuse to record the charge."

The Investigator was on the point of making a remark, but he restrained himself, sighed, and ordered some sparkling water.

Outside, the rain had yielded to the steady advance of the snow: light, swirling, almost unreal, falling in slow motion now, orchestrating its effects. The Investigator gazed at the snowflakes as they hung a moving screen before his eyes. He could barely make out the pediment of the railroad station, and, farther off, the platforms, the tracks, and the waiting trains were no longer visible. It was as if the place where he'd stopped and stood a short while before had abruptly faded away, leaving no trace of his arrival in this new world, where he had to make an effort to get his bearings.

"It's winter today," the Waiter said, uncapping a little bottle of water and placing it on the table. He was looking not at his customer but at the snowflakes. Moreover, he'd spoken without even addressing the Investigator, as if his thought had escaped from his brain and flitted around his head for a bit, like a poor insect resigned to its imminent demise but nevertheless determined to play its role of insect right to the end, even if its performance interests no one and will save it from nothing.

And for a long moment, the Waiter remained like that, standing immobile beside the table, completely ignoring the Investigator, and staring out the window, entranced by the snow, by the milky particles gliding down along their elegant but irrational trajectories.

II

T HE INVESTIGATOR COULD HAVE SWORN he'd seen two
or three taxicabs when he left the train station. Waiting taxis with headlights on and engines running, their
exhaust smoke gray, delicate, quickly vanishing. But the cabs
must all have gone somewhere else; the Investigator imagined the passengers, warm and comfortable on the back seat.
It was really too bad.

The snow had decided to stay awhile and was falling still,
imposing itself like a monarch. The Investigator had asked
the Waiter for directions, expecting a disagreeable response,
but the Waiter had seemed happy to inform him that it really
wasn't difficult at all, the Enterprise was vast, he couldn't
miss it. It spilled over everywhere. Whatever street he took,
it would necessarily lead him to a surrounding wall, a wire-
mesh gate, an entryway, a warehouse, a loading dock belonging to the Enterprise.

"One way or another," the Waiter had added, "*everything*
here more or less belongs to the Enterprise." He'd placed a lot
of emphasis on *everything*. "It's simply a matter of following
the wall," he went on, "and you'll come to the main entrance
and the Guardhouse."

And with that, the Waiter had gone back to his horse

races. His elbows on the bar, his head in his hands, and his eyes fixed on the foaming thoroughbreds as they hurtled across the television screen, he hadn't reacted at all when the Investigator told him good-bye, crossed the threshold of the establishment, and stepped out of his life.

The Waiter's part was at an end anyway.

It wasn't yet night, but the nocturnal atmosphere was nonetheless quite evident, augmented by the total solitude through which the Investigator moved as he walked along snow-covered sidewalks without ever passing a living soul. Only every now and then did he get the feeling that the place was inhabited, and that was when his little silhouette entered the creamy yellow halo shed by a streetlight and remained there briefly, the time required to cover a few yards, before being swallowed up again in the thick, impenetrable shadows.

His suitcase was getting heavier. His raincoat needed wringing out. Ignoring discomfort, the Investigator marched on. He was shivering more and more. His thoughts were wandering around, just like his cold, sore feet. Suddenly he saw himself as a convict, an outlaw, a last survivor, someone looking for shelter after escaping a final catastrophe, whether chemical, ecological, or nuclear. He felt his body becoming his enemy and stepped along in a dream. There didn't seem to be any end of stepping along. He had the impression he'd been roaming hither and thither for hours. All the streets were identical. The snow, in its abstract uniformity, covered up every distinguishing feature. Was he going in circles?

The shock was brief and muffled, but it nevertheless left him quite stunned. He'd collided with a man or maybe a woman—he wasn't sure which—but in any case a human

shape that had erupted out of the night, coming toward
him at a moderate but uncheckable speed. The Investigator
murmured his excuses in a few polite words. From the other
he heard nothing, except some grumbling and the sound of
footsteps moving away. He glimpsed a silhouette before the
night dissolved it.

Another dream?

No, some tangible signs of the incident remained: a sharp
pain in his left shoulder, and a sore spot on his forehead,
which he rubbed as expiring snowflakes ran down his face.
And then there was his suitcase, of course. His suitcase. Burst
open, its contents spread over the ground, reminiscent of the
bags and baggage one sees in news reports, floating on the
surface of the ocean in the aftermath of one plane crash or
another, the final witnesses of lives tossed by the currents, of
lives disappeared, pulverized, annihilated, reduced to sweat-
ers soaked in salt water, to trousers still in movement, even
though the legs they contained are gone, to stuffed animals,
surprised at having lost forever the arms of the children who
held them.

The Investigator experienced some difficulty in gathering up his five shirts, his underwear, his pajamas, his toilet
things, his polyester pants, his alarm clock, several pairs of
socks, a bag (still empty) for his dirty laundry, his electric
razor, and its rebellious cord. During the process, he stepped
on a tube of toothpaste, which spurted out and lay on the
ground like a big pink-and-blue worm, redolent of synthetic
mint. Eventually, he was able to close the suitcase, which was
heavier, because along with his personal items he was now
carrying a little snow, a little rain, a little melancholy.

But it was imperative that he keep on walking. It was by

this time full night, and he was finding the City more and more inhospitable, uninhabited, as it appeared to be, except by the occasional shadow with a body as solid as a bull, capable of staggering a man with a single blow of its horn. And to cap his misfortune, the Investigator launched into the first of three violent sneezes. He was sure he'd wake up the next day with his nose running, his throat dry, raspy, and nearly closed, and his feverish head stuck inside a snare drum. The prospect of such a morning filled him with mild dread. Ah, to wake up feeling like that, he thought, before beginning a long and no doubt tedious day of investigating, what rotten luck!

To wake up, yes. In a room, of course. But what room? Where?

III

SO THIS WAS SUPPOSED TO BE the Guardhouse? But it didn't look anything like a guardhouse, nor did its surroundings look like the entrance to any enterprise whatsoever, much less to the Enterprise itself.

The Investigator had passed the place some three or four times without suspecting that it could be the Guardhouse: a kind of bunker, a massive parallelepiped of raw, unfinished concrete, pierced at irregular intervals by thin, vertical openings as narrow as arrow slits. All these features combined to give the impression of absolute closure. The building designated whoever approached it as an intruder, perhaps even an enemy. The chevaux-de-frise set up on all sides suggested that an attack was imminent and must be parried, and the rolls of barbed wire, the caltrop barriers, and the chicanes that could be glimpsed behind them intensified the general atmosphere of imminent threat. Images of fortified embassies in war-torn countries crossed the Investigator's mind. But the Enterprise wasn't an embassy, and the country wasn't at war. According to the information that had been made available to him, the only things manufactured within these guarded precincts were innocuous communications products and the software to implement them, nothing with any strategic value, and it had been a long time since the production had been carried out in any actual secrecy. There was really no justification for taking such measures as these.

At last, the Investigator found a window on one side of the Guardhouse. There was a counter behind the window, and next to the window a buzzer set into the exterior wall. Behind the counter, on the other side of the thick glass panel—was it bulletproof glass?—a surgical light illuminated a small room, a few dozen square feet in area. The Investigator could see a desk, a chair, a calendar pinned to the back wall, and, higher up, a big display board with several long lines of lights, some on, some off, some blinking. On the left-hand wall, a group of television monitors offered a regular mosaic of views of the Enterprise: offices, warehouses, parking lots, stairways, empty workshops, cellars, loading docks.

The snowfall had stopped. The Investigator was trembling. He couldn't feel his nose anymore. He'd turned up the collar of his raincoat as high as he could in an effort to protect his neck, but the coat was now thoroughly drenched, and the upturned collar only added to his discomfort. He pressed the buzzer. Nothing happened. He pressed it again and waited. He took a look around and called out, but without much hope, because no sound of human origin could be heard, only mechanical noises, the hum of engines or boilers or power stations or generators, which mingled with the rising murmur of the wind as it began to blow harder.

"What is it?"

The Investigator jumped. The crackling, slightly aggressive words had come from an intercom speaker located just to the left of the buzzer.

"Good day," the Investigator managed to say after recovering from his surprise.

"Good evening," answered the voice, which seemed to come from a great distance, from the depths of an infernal world. The Investigator apologized, explained himself, said who he was, recounted his waiting in front of the train station, his stop in the café, the Waiter's directions, his long walk, his mistakes along the way, his repeated passages in front of the . . . The voice interrupted him right in the middle of a sentence.

"Are you in possession of an Exceptional Authorization?"

"Excuse me? I don't understand."

"Are you in possession of an Exceptional Authorization?"

"Exceptional Auth—? I'm the Investigator. . . . I don't know what you're talking about. Surely my visit here has been announced. I'm expected. . . ."

"For the last time, are you in possession, yes or no, of an Exceptional Authorization?"

"No, but I'll surely get one tomorrow"—the Investigator, who was gradually losing his grasp, hesitated—"after I meet with a Manager. . . ."

"Without an Exceptional Authorization, you are not authorized to enter the premises of the Enterprise after 2100 hours."

The Investigator was preparing to reply that it was only . . . But he glanced at his watch and could hardly believe it: almost quarter to ten. How was it possible? So that meant he'd been walking for hours? How could he have lost all sense of time like that?

"I'm confused," he said. "I didn't realize it was so late."

"Come back tomorrow."

The Investigator heard a sound like a cleaver coming down on a butcher's block. The crackling ceased. He started to tremble even harder. His socks, too thin for the season anyway, were soaked through. The bottom parts of his trousers looked like wet rags. His fingers and toes were getting numb. He leaned on the buzzer one more time.

"Now what?" said the distant voice furiously.

"I'm very sorry to disturb you again, but I need a place to spend the night."

"We're not a hotel."

"Exactly, so perhaps you could tell me where to find one?"

"We're not the Tourist Office."

The voice disappeared. This time, the Investigator concluded that it would be useless to ring again. He was seized by a great weariness, and at the same time, panic made his heart beat at an unusually high rate. He placed his hand on his chest and felt, through the layers of wet clothing, the rapid rhythm, the dull blows of the organ against the wall of flesh. It was as if somebody were knocking at a door, an inner door, a closed door, desperately, without ever getting a response, without anyone's ever opening it for him.

THE SITUATION WAS GROWING ABSURD. He'd never had such a strange misadventure. He went so far as to rub his eyes and bite his lips in an effort to persuade himself that the events of the past few hours had not been just a nightmare.

But, no, there he was, all right, standing in front of that entrance that didn't look a thing like an entrance, before the wall surrounding the Enterprise, which didn't look like any other enterprise, next to a Guardhouse completely different from an ordinary guardhouse, standing there with chattering teeth, drenched to the bone, at ten o'clock in the evening—no, later—while the rain, no doubt with a view to increasing his amazement, routed the snow again and started hammering on his skull.

He hauled rather than carried his suitcase, which no longer contained only his clothes and other personal items; now there were stones in it, steel beams, chunks of cast iron, blocks of granite. Each of his steps was accompanied by a squelching sound, like the sound a sponge makes when you squeeze it. The sidewalks were turning into great swamps. He wouldn't have been all that surprised if he'd suddenly been seized and dragged down by the deep current of some

bottomless puddle. But all at once, a memory crossed his
mind and rekindled his hope. He recalled a moment, during the course of his wandering, when he'd looked down the
length of a street and spotted—on the right, he remembered
it had been on the right, but what good was that piece of
information going to do him?—in any case, he'd spotted an
illuminated sign, and he believed (but here he abandoned
the realm of certainty; this wasn't a belief he'd stake his life
on) that the sign was a hotel sign. He was sure there would
be plenty of hotels on the periphery of the City, on its noisy
edges, where freeway interchanges performed their function,
purging the fast lanes of excessive traffic, bleeding arteries
clogged with vehicles, separating destinies and lives. But at
this hour, there was no question of his attempting to reach
those conjectural hotels on foot, and in such weather. To
begin with, what would be the right way for him to go? He
hadn't the least idea.

And to think, a very simple act could have saved him all
this trouble: Had he thought to recharge his cell phone before
leaving his apartment that morning, he'd already be asleep
in a nice, warm bed, listening to the rain drumming on the
roof of the hotel, which he would have found with no problem, simply by dialing for information. But the small, inert,
useless object in his raincoat pocket—he could feel it now
and then, when he passed his suitcase from one hand to the
other—reminded him of his negligence and his stupidity.

What time could it be? He didn't dare consult his watch
again. He was exhausted and chilled through and through.
He sneezed every three yards, and fluid ran from his nose
like tepid water from a treacherous and badly closed faucet.
He wasn't going to be forced to sleep in the train station or

on a bench, like a homeless person, was he? In any case, that was a moot point, because he remembered that train stations all over the country now chained up their doors at night, precisely to avoid being turned into dormitories; moreover, public benches installed during the last several years were designed in such a way that you couldn't lie on them anymore.

He walked on at random; by now, nothing looked familiar. He crossed intersections, tramped past buildings, traversed neighborhoods of low-rise, detached houses with no light on in any window. Could it be that not a soul was awake in the entire City? The streets were empty of vehicles: no cars, no motorcycles, no bicycles. Nothing. It was as if a curfew were in force, and it forbade traffic of any kind.

The Waiter had told him the truth: The Enterprise was always with him. He could distinguish, near and far, the somber conglomeration of its facilities; seen through the streaks of freezing rain, the structures formed ramparts and high walls, sometimes crenellated, always thick and oppressive. And then there was the sound the Enterprise made, audible in spite of the raindrops striking the pavement: a noticeable, continuous, low whirring, like the sound a refrigerator makes when its door has been left open.

The Investigator felt old and discouraged, even though his Investigation hadn't begun yet, even though nothing had actually begun. The rain doubled its force, as did the wind, which swept the streets methodically, exhaling a kind of earthy, fetid, glacial breath that just about finished him off. He'd been walking for . . . for how long, really? He didn't have any idea, and now he was in a part of the City where there were no buildings. The sidewalks were lined by a concrete fence about ten feet high, on the top of which glittered innumerable pieces of broken glass set in cement. The narrow streets, which forked repeatedly, reinforced his unpleasant sensation that he'd become a kind of rodent, caught in an outsized trap. The monotonous and restrictive landscape completed his disorientation, but he kept moving. He had the curious impression that he was being observed by an invisible creature located somewhere very high above him and laughing heartily at the wretchedness of his state.

A T FIRST, HE TOLD HIMSELF that exhaustion was causing him to see mirages. And then the name on the unlit sign—HOPE HOTEL—comforted him with the thought that someone—a kind of game-master—was playing a little trick on him and observing his reaction with a subtle smile. He nearly wept for joy, but instead he burst out laughing, loudly and at some length. True, the sign was off—was this the one he thought he'd seen lit up a few hours earlier?—but the place was indeed a hotel, a real hotel, modest-looking, probably a little creaky, judging from its decrepit façade and the flaking paint on its shutters, some of which were hanging from only one hinge, but nonetheless an active hotel, with a plaque indicating the category of the establishment— four stars! Its façade merited only one, if that—and a notice displaying the prohibitive prices of the rooms. Through the glass doors he could see the apparently tidy lobby, as well as the tiny lamp whose tiny light faintly illuminated a sort of counter, to the left of which he could make out several dozen keys of various sizes hanging from butcher's hooks.

The Investigator, who had practically run across the street when he saw the Hotel, searched a little breathlessly for the night bell, but after several minutes came to the conclusion that there wasn't any. Still, he was now certain that his ordeal was almost over, and he didn't care how much he had to pay. He was prepared to disburse a fortune in exchange for a warm, dry room and a bed to lie on. There would be time tomorrow to look around for a hotel better suited to his means.

He knocked on the door—gently, discreetly—and waited. Nothing happened. He knocked again, a bit harder this time. It crossed his mind that the Night Clerk wasn't doing very much in the way of clerking. The Investigator imagined him plunged into a deep, comalike slumber. Was it possible that there was no one on duty? He shivered and began to yell, pounding on the door in a sudden burst of energy. The Hope Hotel remained hopelessly closed and mute. The Investigator let himself slide down the door like a heavy sandbag. He collapsed onto his suitcase, which he clutched as though it were a loved one or a life preserver—a strange life preserver indeed, as wet as the waves it was supposed to save him from.

"What do you want?"

He jerked his head up. The door of the Hotel was open, and a woman was standing close beside him, a very tall, very fat woman. To the Investigator, who was lying in a heap on the ground, for all the world like an insect or a reptile, she seemed a veritable giantess, a giantess in the act of tying a belt around her pink, fraying terry-cloth bathrobe. She looked at him in amazement. He mumbled some words of apology, managed to rise to his feet, smoothed his raincoat and trousers, wiped his tears and his nose with the back of his hand, sniffled, and then, at last, instinctively coming to attention, almost like a soldier, he introduced himself: "I'm the Investigator."

"So?" the Giantess replied, not giving him time to go on. Her large body gave off a slight scent of perspiration as well as a tepid warmth, the warmth of the bed from which she'd been roused by his racket. Since she hadn't drawn her robe all the way around her, the Investigator could see the lighter fabric of her nightgown and its washed-out pattern of daisies and daffodils. Her features were blurry with sleep, and the thick coils of her bright-red hair were skewered on a long, haphazardly inserted hairpin.

"Would you by chance have an available room?" the Investigator asked, not without some difficulty. He didn't yet dare to think that his grotesque ordeal might be coming to an end.

"A room!" the Giantess said, speaking distinctly and opening her eyes wide, as if his request were absurd, inappropriate, possibly even obscene. The Investigator once again felt his legs buckling under him. She looked shocked and outraged.

"Yes, a room," he replied, and it was almost a supplication.

"Do you know what time it is?"

He dared to shrug his shoulders a little. "Yes . . ." he murmured, though he hadn't the least idea how late it was or the nerve to look at his watch. He lacked even the strength to apologize, and he shrank from launching into an explication that wouldn't have been very convincing in any case and might possibly have aroused yet more suspicion.

The Giantess thought for a few seconds, grumbling. In the end she said, "Follow me!"

THE GIANTESS HAD HIM FILL OUT an incalculable number of forms. As soon as he finished each one, she tried
to put the information on the hard drive of an old computer, but she looked uncomfortable at the keyboard, typing
with two fingers, often hitting the wrong key, and closing the
program inadvertently no fewer than five times before she
was able to save the data; she had to start over from scratch
every time.

At last, she handed him a copy of the Hotel Rules—a single sheet, printed on both sides, sealed in plastic, and covered
with fingerprints that made the text illegible in places—
and required him to read them aloud, carefully, in front of
her. Because he wished to be agreeable, he didn't balk at her
request.

Afterward, she took the trouble to verify that he'd
retained and digested what he'd read by quizzing him about
it: "Is smoking allowed in the rooms?" "From when to
when is breakfast served?" "Where?" "Are Guests allowed
to receive visitors from outside the Hotel in their rooms?"
"What is it strictly forbidden to throw into the toilets?" and
so on.

When he gave the wrong answer to her fourteenth question—"Are Guests permitted to iron their personal belongings in their rooms without first informing the Management?"—the Giantess requested that he reread the Rules in their entirety, all thirty-four paragraphs. The thought of being shown to the door and forced to finish the night in the street convinced the Investigator that he should do as she said. In the end, he managed to pass the test, and the Giantess allowed him to choose one of the keys on the board, having first asked him for a piece of identification and his credit card, which she'd then proceeded to shut up, before he had time to protest, in a little box situated below the board with the keys, all in accordance with paragraph 18, line C of the Rules, which stated that in cases of nocturnal arrival, the Management of the Hope Hotel reserved the right to keep the Guest's identification papers and credit card or other means of payment as a security deposit until the forenoon of the following day.

"Pick one fast. I'm in no mood to wait much longer. It's 3:16 a.m., my nights are short, and I can't wait to get back in bed!"

He settled on number 14. The Giantess took the key off its hook and without a word began to climb the stairs. The Investigator followed her.

He tripped and nearly fell on the very first stair, because its unusually tall riser contradicted his unconscious muscle memory, and he didn't step high enough. By contrast, the next stair was very low, too low, which likewise disoriented him and nearly led to a fall. The result was that he began to pay strict attention, despite his fatigue, to every step, telling himself that in any case there weren't going to be fifty of them; room number 14, the room he'd chosen, must be on the second floor, so there couldn't be many more stairs to go.

His concentration paid off, and he climbed on without stumbling. Given that no two risers were the same height, he was pleased with his performance, but he thought that only a lunatic could have constructed such a stairway. Long after he and his escort had passed the second floor, they kept climbing, climbing, climbing. On the point of collapse, the Investigator gritted his teeth and toiled upward behind the Giantess. He lugged his suitcase along as best he could, ascending floor after floor, one step at a time. The Hotel seemed like an infinite tower whose apparent purpose was to pierce the sky, as a hand drill's reason for being is to put holes in wood.

Then, with brutal abruptness, a thought came to him, a luminous, self-evident, indubitable thought: He was dead. He'd died without noticing it. This struck him as the obvious explanation; what other could there be? Maybe it had happened a few hours before, right after he got off the train. Maybe he'd inadvertently walked across some tracks. Maybe a freight train had struck him, crushed him, reduced him to nothing. Or maybe the event—a catastrophic collapse, a heart attack, a massive stroke—had taken place earlier, as he was leaving the Director's office with his new orders and just after he said hello to the Accountant, who was standing by the vending machine, fixing her hair and makeup while waiting for a cup of coffee. Or maybe he'd died at home. In the morning, when he first woke up, even before shutting off the vibrating alarm clock with its hands pointing to 6:15. An instantaneous, painless death. A long slide. And after that, nothing. Or, rather, yes, something: namely, this nightmare, which must be a kind of stress test, an initiation ordeal, an upgraded purgatory. Somewhere, someone was observing him, he was more and more sure of it. Someone was studying him. Someone was going to determine his lot.

"Here it is," the Giantess said. "And there's your key." She handed him the object in question—he found it quite heavy—adjusted the front of her robe, lightly passed her right hand over her forehead, which was speckled with fine beads of sweat, and went back down the stairs without so much as wishing him a good night, carrying off with her her somnolent, animal smell. The Investigator inserted the key into the lock and turned it, expecting it not to work.

He was, however, wrong. He entered the room quickly, put down his suitcase, didn't even look for the light switch, felt around until he came to a piece of furniture shaped like a bed, dropped onto it fully dressed, and—after breathing heavily for several minutes, like a man saved from drowning by big, ruddy, clumsy hands—fell asleep.

A SOUND LIKE AN OCEAN LINER'S SIREN—an enormous sound that shrieked for three or four seconds, stopped, and then began again—flung him out of his sleep. He sat up in the bed, searched in vain for a light switch, and struck his forehead against an object attached to the wall. The object fell with a great crash, the whooping of the siren immediately ceased, and then he heard a voice, a voice that was at once near and far.

"Hello! Hello? Hello, can you hear me . . . ? Hello?"

The Investigator groped around in the dark and took hold of the telephone receiver, which was hanging at the end of its cord. "Yes, I can hear you."

"Hello! Can you hear me?" the voice repeated anxiously.

"I can hear you," the Investigator said again, a little louder this time. "Who are you?"

"Hello!!" the voice yelled. *"Hello!!!"*

"Go ahead! I can hear you! I can hear you perfectly!"

"Goddamn it! Is someone there or not? Answer me, please! I beg you, answer me! I'm locked in! I've been locked in!!! I can't get out of this room!" The voice had taken on the accents of great despair.

"I'm here! I'm here," the Investigator said. "I can hear you perfectly!"

At the other end of the line, the voice yelled one more time, there was a crackling sound, and then nothing more, except for an intermittent and unpleasant dial tone.

The Investigator ran both hands over the wall above the bed until he finally found the light switch. After a few hesitant blinks, the ceiling light came on. It was a circular neon tube that filled the room with a green glow and revealed it to be much bigger than the Investigator had thought. The bed he lay on seemed lost in the vast space, which measured at least thirty feet by twenty. He was stunned for a few seconds. Aside from the bed, the furniture consisted of a very small wardrobe wedged into one corner and a chair placed in the middle of the room, directly under the ceiling light. There was nothing else. No night table. No desk. The old parquet floor was covered here and there by faded Oriental rugs that had lost their colors and their patterns. On the back wall was a photograph, a picture of an old man with a mustache. The Investigator had the feeling he'd seen that face before, but he wasn't certain. He looked around. This place certainly didn't provide the décor and comfort of a four-star hotel!

The Investigator glanced at his watch: 6:45. That mistaken telephone call had been a good thing, after all. Without it, God only knew when he would have waked up! But the crazy person who'd called him—who could he have been?

He got out of bed. He'd slept for only a few hours. His head hurt, and his nose, which was swollen, hot, and bruised, wouldn't stop running. He shivered as he realized that he hadn't even taken off his raincoat, which was somewhat drier, though far from dry, and totally wrinkled. His crumpled suit gave off a strange odor of wild mushrooms, his shirt looked like a rag, and his tie had coiled itself three times around his throat. His shoes—he'd kept them on, too—were still soaked.

He undressed rapidly, placed his clothes, including undershirt and -pants, on the bed, and headed for a door that he supposed led to the bathroom. The proportions of this latter space left him dumbfounded: It was a narrow closet. As the Hotel room itself was uselessly large, so the bathroom was amazingly small, cramped, low-ceilinged, and of dubious cleanliness to boot. Hairs short and long in the washbasin bore witness to a previous guest whose traces no one had taken the trouble to erase. The Investigator bent forward slightly and entered the bathroom. Fear of never being able to open the door again kept him from closing it behind him. Moving sideways and with a great deal of effort, he managed to penetrate what served as a shower. Since he was unable to turn around, he slipped his left hand behind his back and turned on the faucet; a jet of icy water struck him between the shoulder blades. He couldn't stop himself from crying out. Groping blindly behind him, he located the lever that adjusted the water temperature; the result of his manipulations was a barrage of scalding water, which turned icy again when he moved the lever in the opposite direction. The Investigator opted for cold, forcing himself to bear the torture for nearly thirty seconds before turning off the faucet and wriggling out of the shower.

He dried himself with the help of a minuscule hand towel and then gazed into the narrow mirror above the similarly narrow washbasin. The reflection he saw there was a deformed and monstrous version of himself. Apparently, when he banged into the base of the wall telephone, he'd opened a cut in his forehead more than an inch long. The cut had bled profusely. He cleaned away the blood, but he was left with a deep, open wound, an unsightly gash. One might have thought he'd been struck in a fight or someone had tried to knock him out.

Not without difficulty, he squeezed out of the bathroom, took his electric razor from his suitcase, slipped back into the narrow space, and got down on all fours in order to plug the razor's cord into the outlet, which—and this was almost diabolical—was located behind the pedestal supporting the washbasin and almost level with the floor. At last, with the plug successfully inserted, he pressed the "on" button.

Nothing.

He made sure the cord was properly attached to the razor and tried again.

Nothing.

He looked around the Hotel room for another electrical outlet and ended up finding one, half hidden by the little wardrobe. This he pushed to one side, thereby exposing the outlet as well as several mounds of dust, a couple of cigarette butts, three used tissues, and an old dental retainer. He plugged in the razor and turned it on: still nothing. His razor refused to work. The Investigator remembered how, early in the previous evening's long expedition, his suitcase had opened and spilled its contents on the sidewalk. The razor must have struck the ground, or perhaps its motor had gotten wet. He placed it on the radiator under the window. The radiator was working, but not very hard; it was barely warm.

From his supply of five shirts, he chose the least wet and then pulled on his other pair of trousers. Unfortunately, he had only the one suit jacket. He tried to smooth out its wrinkles with the flat of his hand, but without much success, and despite a pair of clean, practically dry socks, putting on his soggy shoes proved to be thoroughly disagreeable. He tied his tie, whose edges were curling up, and then raised his right hand to pat down his surviving wisps of hair. He was ready to go downstairs and get his breakfast.

But first, he wanted to let some air into his room and thus disperse the heavy odor of dampness and soaked leather that had permeated it. He pushed aside the double curtains, had a hard time pulling the window open, managed to draw the rusty metal latch that held the two shutters together, placed a palm on each one, and pushed them both at once; they moved no more than an absurd half-inch or so. The Investigator exerted more pressure, but the result was the same. It was incomprehensible. It felt as though the shutters were butting up against something harder than they were. He brought his face closer, peered between the slats, and discovered that large concrete blocks, carefully set in courses and mortared, prevented the shutters from opening.

The situation was obvious, and he had to face it: He was in a room with a walled-up window.

A FTER SEARCHING IN VAIN for an elevator, the Investigator walked down the stairs, wondering as he did so
what kind of place he'd landed in. Its obscenely high
room rates were those of a luxury hotel, and yet it offered
the quality and comfort of a squalid dump scheduled for
demolition.

Seventy-three. That was the number of steps he'd gone
down. Six floors already and he still hadn't reached the lobby.
As a way of avoiding all other thoughts, he concentrated on
making an accurate count. Total silence reigned in the Hotel.
The only lights in the stairwell were dim bulbs fixed to the
wall at long intervals from one another, so long that going
downstairs proved to be a dangerous endeavor.

The Investigator finally stepped onto the ground floor,
having counted nine floors down. So his room, number 14,
was located on the ninth floor. The management apparently
did not allow itself to be burdened by logic. But after all, he
told himself, was the world he lived in logical? Wasn't logic
just a purely mathematical concept, a kind of postulate no
proof had ever confirmed?

There was no one behind the reception counter, but a strip
of light showed under the door that the Giantess had pointed

out as the entrance to the breakfast room. He walked over to the door, seized and turned the handle—thus producing an unpleasant squeal, a sound like human wailing—and pushed the door open.

Then he froze in the doorway.

The room was a very large hall whose other end he could barely make out, but what most astonished him was the fact that this vast space was packed with humanity. Although there were countless tables, he didn't see an unoccupied chair at any of them. Hundreds of people were having breakfast, and all of them suspended their gestures and interrupted their conversations when the Investigator entered. Hundreds of eyes looked him over. He felt his face turning crimson. He prepared to utter some kind of apology, a few words, perhaps a general greeting, but he didn't have time. After the several seconds of total silence that accompanied his entrance, the noise returned and filled the room again, a thousand noises, in fact, a veritable din of words and masticating jaws and throats swallowing liquids and breakfast rolls, the clinking and clanking of cups and saucers and glasses and chairs. He had yet to get over his surprise when a Server wearing a white coat and black pants appeared beside him.

"You're in number 14?"

"Yes . . ." the Investigator said, stuttering a little.

"Please follow me."

The Server led him halfway across the room. The meandering course they took allowed the Investigator to note that all the people sitting at the tables were speaking a foreign language—Slavic perhaps, unless it was Scandinavian or Middle Eastern.

"There you are, sir!" the Server said to him, pointing to

an empty chair at a table for four. The other three seats were occupied by men with low foreheads, dark skin, and thick black hair. They bent over their cups, drinking and eating greedily.

The Investigator sat down. The Server awaited his order.

"I'll have a cup of tea, some toast, and orange juice, please."

"Tea, yes. Toast and orange juice, no."

"Why not? At the rate I'm paying! Isn't this supposed to be a four-star establishment?"

"You haven't paid anything yet," the Server pointed out dryly. "And the fact that this Hotel has four stars doesn't give you unlimited rights, and especially not the right to behave like a person to whom everything is due."

The Investigator was flabbergasted and incapable of replying. The Server turned to go, but the Investigator held him back. "Excuse me," the Investigator said. "I'd like to ask you a question."

The Server said nothing, but he didn't go away, either. The Investigator thought this an encouraging sign. He said, "I just got here last night, and it seems to me, well, I believe your colleague, a tall woman in a bathrobe, I believe she gave me to understand that the Hotel was empty, and this morning I see that—"

"Tourists. There was a sudden, massive arrival of Tourists."

"Tourists?" the Investigator repeated, remembering the depressing, unlovely streets he'd walked for hours in rain and snow, the endless wall, the gray buildings, the monstrous bulk of the Enterprise's innumerable structures, the absence of all charm, all beauty.

"Our City attracts many Tourists," the Server snapped. This declaration stunned the Investigator, and the Server, taking advantage of the ensuing silence, withdrew.

The Investigator unfolded his napkin and looked at his table companions, who continued to eat and drink. "Good day!" the Investigator greeted them.

None of the men replied or even looked up. The Server returned. He placed two rusks and a cup of black coffee in front of him and then went away before the Investigator had a chance to tell him that rusks and coffee were not at all what he'd ordered.

IX

THE RUSKS TASTED LIKE HUMUS. As for the black coffee, it was beyond the shadow of a doubt the bitterest the Investigator had ever drunk in his life, and not even the copious amount of sugar he added succeeded in sweetening it. His three neighbors were devouring cheese omelets, cold cuts, smoked fish, large pickles marinated in vinegar, apple-and-cinnamon pastries, small, soft rolls of bread stuffed with raisins and almonds, and fresh fruit. They were drinking grapefruit juice, pineapple juice, and black tea whose delicious fragrance, full-bodied and smoky, entered the Investigator's nostrils.

His table companions kept up a lively conversation, but the Investigator was unable to understand a single word. None of the others paid any attention to him.

He forced himself to drink his coffee, figuring that the hot liquid would do him good. He felt feverish and couldn't stop blowing his nose. From time to time, he raised his eyes and looked around, trying to spot the Giantess, but she was nowhere in sight. There were only four or five Servers working in the big room, men who looked so much alike—short, somewhat round, balding—that they could have been taken for brothers. The Tourists, as he'd decided to call them, were making an unbelievable racket. They were all simply dressed men and women of around forty, and they were eating grossly, flinging themselves upon the abundant repast set before them. The Investigator determined that he was the only Guest who'd been served the rudimentary breakfast he was forcing himself to swallow, so when a Server passed near him, he asked whether he, too, could have an omelet and some fruit juice.

"Are you part of the group?"

"No, I'm—"

"Are you in room 14?"

"Yes."

"I'm very sorry, but it's not possible."

"Come on, that's ridiculous! Can't you at least give me a little jam, or just some butter? If it's only a matter of money, I'll pay the additional charge. . . ."

"Don't insist. In here, money doesn't solve all problems."

When the Investigator recovered from his shock and surprise, the Server was already far away. In his head, the Investigator reviewed all the articles contained in the Hotel Rules; he'd read them twice upon his arrival, and he didn't remember a single one that made any reference at all to any sort of discrimination in regard to breakfast. He promised himself to point this out to someone in the Management as soon as he came across such a person.

Time was passing. The Investigator was reminded of this by an enormous wall clock, which punctuated every movement of its second hand with a resounding crack, like a hammer striking an anvil. He shouldn't drag his heels. People must be waiting for him and growing impatient. He picked up his cup to finish his coffee, but just as he was bringing the cup to his mouth, his neighbor hit his elbow. The coffee spilled on him, on his coat and trousers. The Investigator cursed as he watched two dark-brown stains spreading over the light fabric. The man who had caused this disaster didn't apologize. He kept eating and talking to the two others, who likewise acted as though the Investigator didn't exist.

The Investigator rose from the table and walked rapidly toward a door under a sign that read TOILETS. He was beside himself. He'd had enough and more than enough, he thought, and he wondered whether he shouldn't take the next train home. But what could he say to his Head of Section? How would he explain his premature return before the Investigation had taken place, before it had even begun? Would he say that he'd wandered around the City for hours in filthy weather? That he'd found the Hotel strange? That the breakfast he'd been served hadn't suited him? That the coffee was dreadful? That the conduct of the Hotel staff was unacceptable? That his table companions hadn't spoken to him?

No, it was a better idea to be patient.

The corridor he'd entered from the breakfast room dead-ended some ten yards away. There were two doors in the wall on his left. On the first one, a pictogram showed a female silhouette; he went on to the second, but it was adorned with the same image. He retraced his steps, thinking he was mistaken. No. He'd seen right. Both doors indicated that they led to ladies' rooms. The Investigator felt his heart shift gears. The joke was still on him.

He shot a glance to left and right and even above his head. Nobody. Without hesitating a second longer, he went in. The restroom was deserted. He went over to a sink, turned on the hot water, and dug in his pocket for his handkerchief, which wasn't there. Or in his other pocket, either.

A continuous cloth towel was hanging from a roller. The Investigator tried to pull the towel down gently, but without success. He pulled on the cloth again, then harder, then harder still. The towel tore, the screw fixing the roller to the plaster wall came loose, and a mesh of fine cracks appeared on the plaster. He wet the towel and applied it energetically to the two coffee stains. After a few minutes, it seemed to him that their dark color was fading a little; however, though the stains were lighter, they now covered a larger area. The Investigator threw the towel into a trash can, pushing the wet, torn cloth down to the bottom of the can and covering it with paper. Then he left the restroom.

When he pushed open the door to the breakfast room, the hubbub had completely ceased, and the Tourists, without exception, had disappeared. All the tables had been cleared and tidied up; not a speck of refuse remained. How was this possible, when he'd been gone for four minutes at the most?

The chairs had been resituated and carefully aligned. He looked at his place. The coffee cup was still there, as well as the second rusk, which he hadn't finished eating. On the chair, which was slightly askew with respect to the table, he saw his raincoat. It was the only table in the room that showed any sign of the recent breakfast.

The Servers themselves had become invisible.

The Investigator hurried over to his place. He wanted to get out of that room as soon as possible, and out of the Hotel, too; he wanted to go outside and take a few deep breaths of fresh air and feel its coolness on his temples, on the back of his neck, in his lungs, in his brain, as it were, his brain, which was being tried and tested, so severely that the Investigator wondered whether it might not simply explode. But just as he was putting on his raincoat, feeling once again its extremely unpleasant dampness, he heard a powerful voice at his back, calling to him from rather far away.

"You're not going to finish your breakfast?"

X

H E FROZE IN PLACE AND THEN, very slowly, with fear in his belly, turned around. A man was coming toward him, a man who was neither a Server nor a Tourist. The closer he approached, the clearer his outline and features became. He looked as though he might be around the same age as the Investigator, and the same size, too. He was smiling.

"You're not going to finish your breakfast?" the man repeated, gesturing toward the cup and the rusk. His voice was friendly.

"I'm not very hungry anymore," the Investigator mumbled. "And I'm already late."

"Late? If you say so. My feeling about life is, we're often early, and death always comes too soon. Come, sit down, finish your breakfast calmly, don't worry about me."

The Investigator didn't have the strength to protest. There was something imperious beneath the man's bonhomie. Without removing his raincoat—into which he'd slipped only one arm—the Investigator sat down. The man took the opposite chair and looked attentively at the Investigator.

"Did you sleep well?"

"I arrived very late, and—"

"I know," the man said, interrupting him. "The night was short. But eat, please. Pretend I don't exist!"

The man pointed to the remaining rusk. The Investigator picked it up reluctantly and began to nibble at it.

"Let me introduce myself," said the man. "I'm the Policeman."

"The Policeman . . . ?" the Investigator repeated fearfully. He put his rusk down and shook the hand the other man held out to him.

"Exactly. And you are . . ."

"I have," the Investigator started to reply, choking a little and sweating a lot, "that is to say, I am . . . I am . . ."

"You are?"

"I've come to conduct an Investigation into the Enterprise."

"An Investigation? Well, I'll be! An Investigation! And I don't even know anything about it?"

The Policeman maintained his friendly smile throughout, but his eyes stayed fixed on the Investigator's eyes.

"It's not a police investigation, not at all," the Investigator stammered. "Don't get the wrong idea! It's simply a question of administrative procedure. During the past year, the Enterprise has experienced a relatively high—to speak frankly, a most unusually high—number of suicides, and I've been ch—"

"Suicides?" the other interrupted him again.

"Yes. Suicides."

"How many?"

"Around twenty."

"Twenty? And I haven't been informed? But that's incredible! I'm the Policeman, serial suicide is being committed a few steps from my office, and I don't know a thing about it! When you say 'around twenty,' how many do you mean exactly?"

As he grew more and more uncomfortable, the Investigator kept a tight hold on his rusk. He was now sure he had a fever. His head hurt. His eyes stung. His neck was stiff. His nose was hot and painful, as was the cut on his forehead. His whole body made him suffer. The Policeman rummaged in his right coat pocket, then in his left, and extracted a yellow-and-blue medicine bottle, which he handed to the Investigator.

"Take two of these."

"What are they?"

"You have a headache, don't you?"

"How do you know that?"

"I know everything, it's my business. Your arrival yesterday, your visit to the bar, the dispute over the rum toddy, your persistence at the Guardhouse, your banging on the door of the Hotel, then your inability to answer some simple questions concerning the rules of the establishment, and this morning your rude comments on the breakfast. I know about all of it. The dossier I've been given is most thorough. I'm the Policeman. As such, I know. You're the Investigator, so you don't know; you seek. I'm a good distance ahead of you. I said two."

"I beg your pardon?"

"Two tablets. Go ahead and take them, you've still got a little coffee."

The Investigator was holding the medicine bottle in the palm of his hand. He hesitated to open it. The Policeman burst out laughing.

"Come on, don't be afraid! I'm the Policeman, not the Murderer. Everyone has a role, and your role is to be the Investigator, isn't it? And if you pay attention to the proper dosage, there's no risk whatsoever."

The Investigator slowly assented.

"That's the way. Excellent, excellent! Pretend I'm not here." Having said this, the Policeman lowered his head and ostentatiously inspected his hands, as though to demonstrate that he wasn't keeping the Investigator under surveillance. Still totally confounded by the other's sudden arrival and unsure how to react to him, the Investigator ended up opening the medicine bottle and taking out two tablets. Like the bottle, they were yellow and blue. The Investigator examined them closely and tried to sniff them, but his nose was so stopped up that his sense of smell was completely gone. He hesitated a little longer, shut his eyes, and swallowed the pills, washing them down with what remained of the repulsive black coffee.

The Policeman raised his head and looked at the Investigator again, still smiling. "Now, about those suicides. How many, exactly?"

"Twenty-three. But there's some doubt about one of them. It's not known whether the person took his own life or whether his death was an accident. Gas."

"Gas? Radical! You die, and sometimes you take others with you. Was that the case?"

"No. He lived alone in a detached house."

"Too bad . . ."

"I beg your pardon?"

"Nothing. Forget it."

There was silence for a while. The Policeman, although

he continued to smile, appeared to be weighing what the Investigator had just told him about the suicides. Then he made a little hand movement, as if banishing those thoughts and moving on to something else.

"I suppose you think you've landed in a most peculiar place, right?"

"Well, I mean, I must confess—"

A burst of loud laughter from the Policeman startled him. "Sh, sh," the Policeman said. "You don't have to confess anything. This is a conversation we're having, not an interrogation. Relax!"

The Investigator didn't know exactly why, but even though he'd done absolutely nothing he could reproach himself for, a great weight was abruptly lifted from him. He started laughing with the Policeman. It did him good. Oh yes, it really did him good to laugh with this man—a kindly fellow, when all was said and done, and as surprised as he was by the way things had gone.

"I can tell you the whole story," the Investigator said, taking up the conversation again. "But please indulge me, I don't understand it very well myself. I have the impression that I've been living a sort of nightmare ever since I set foot in this town, or, rather, that I'm the victim of a gigantic hoax. Everything seems arranged to prevent me from doing what I have to do. . . ."

"The Investigation into the suicides?"

"Exactly. It's as if . . . What I'm about to say is going to sound absurd, but it's as if everything here, in this town, including the layout of the streets, the absence of signs, the climate—it's as if everything were conspiring to prevent me from carrying out my Investigation, or to delay it as long as possible. I've never known anything like it. And this Hotel! Has anyone ever seen such a hotel?"

The Policeman reflected intensely for a few moments. His round face kept its smile, but his eyes seemed to narrow in fierce concentration.

"When I arrived, I felt the same way you do," he said. "I haven't been here very long. We're constantly being bounced from one post to another, and we obviously can't complain, we don't have the right to complain. I asked myself why I was here. I wondered who could have made the absurd decision to send me to this place, and for what purpose. Of course, I knew I was the Policeman, but I hadn't been given any more precise information about what I was to do or what role I was desired to play. Very strange. Very, very strange. And besides—I'm not sure how to say this—I had an impression, a very distinct impression of a . . . of a presence."

"As if someone were observing you?"

"Exactly. That's just what I mean! But I've never been able to catch anybody at it."

"It's the same with me. I've had that very feeling since yesterday evening."

"Well, in the end, one gets used to it. After all, it's man's nature to adapt, isn't it? And these days, aren't we all constantly under surveillance, wherever we are and whatever we're doing?"

The two men became pensive. Silence reigned until a telephone started ringing. Without hesitation, they simultaneously began to reach into their pockets, which made them both laugh. Then the Investigator remembered that his phone battery was completely discharged. The Policeman pulled out his own device, a kind of mobile phone the Investigator had never seen before: oblong in shape, and equipped with a single button. The Policeman mimicked an apology and pressed the button.

"Yes?"

The Investigator felt relieved. The man across from him, who resembled him in many ways, was a source of comfort.

"Well, what do you know. . . . I see . . ." said the Policeman, taking a notebook and a pen from his pocket. The smile had vanished from his face.

"And what time was that, you said?"

He jotted down a few notes.

"Are you certain?"

The Investigator turned his eyes away so as not to bother his companion.

"Very well. Thank you for informing me."

The Policeman pressed the single button on his telephone and slowly slipped it into one of his pockets. He reread the notes he'd just taken, scratching the back of his neck all the while, and then, with a sharp gesture, he snapped the notebook closed. His eyes were now a fox's eyes, very thin, yellow-brown, and shining.

"Nothing serious, I hope?" asked the Investigator, keeping his tone light.

"That depends on for whom," the Policeman coldly replied. He went on at once, speaking tersely in a metallic voice and stressing every word: "Can you explain to me why, at 7:21 a.m. today, you entered the women's restroom and there willfully destroyed a cloth towel as well as the wood-and-metal structure supporting it, in an act of unjustifiable violence?"

The rusk the Investigator was holding between his fingers exploded into a thousand pieces, and at the same time, he had the sensation that he'd been seized by two strong hands, which were in the act of flinging him down into a bottomless abyss.

XI

Y THE TIME THE INVESTIGATOR WAS finally able to leave
the Hope Hotel, the morning was well advanced.

The Policeman had detained him for more than two
hours, compelling him to answer a barrage of brusque questions. Some of these the Policeman had repeated again and
again, at intervals of a few minutes, in order to make sure
the Investigator's responses didn't vary. He'd been required
to explain, three times and in meticulous detail, his every
action and reaction, no matter how insignificant, since the
moment he'd awakened that morning. He'd had to describe
the telephone call that had rousted him from his sleep, his
discovery of the walled-up window ("I'll verify that," the
Policeman had assured him, almost threateningly), the
counting of the stairs, the massive presence of Tourists in
the breakfast room ("Tourists? Really? First I've heard of
them!" the Policeman had sneered), and, finally, the incident
in the ladies' room.

In addition, the Policeman had insisted on examining,
with the most minute attention, the cut on the Investigator's
forehead. Having completed the examination—for which
he'd pulled on a pair of surgical gloves—the Policeman had

stood erect and ordered the Investigator to accompany him to the restroom for a re-enactment.

"A what?"

"You understood me perfectly well."

"But you must be crazy! A re-enactment for a torn towel? What kind of world is this? I can't waste my time on such childishness. I've got a job to do, an Investigation to conduct. People have died. Men and women have killed themselves. I don't think you realize what suicide represents, but whether you do or not, it is my duty to understand why these acts have been committed. I need to know why, inside such a brief span of time, and within the same enterprise—within the Enterprise—so many people have fallen so deeply into despair that they've chosen to end it all rather than consult a Psychologist or seek help from an Occupational Physician or apply for an appointment with the Director of Human Resources or confide in a colleague or a family member or even to call up one of the many associations that offer assistance to suffering people! And you put obstacles in my path, you detain me for trivialities, you interrogate me for an hour about a mutilated towel, about damages that would never have taken place if this Hotel provided the minimal level of services that a guest has every right to expect, you waste my time with—"

"Who am I?" the Policeman interrupted him.

"You're . . . you told me you were the Policeman."

"Exactly. Well, then?"

"Well, then, what?"

"Well, then! Does one question the Policeman's orders?"

The Investigator opened his mouth, only to feel his throat

dry up and his words die unspoken. His shoulders slumped. "Let's get it over with," he sighed.

The Policeman invited the Investigator to follow him to the ladies' room, where the re-enactment took place. It lasted twenty-seven minutes. The Investigator was obliged to reconstruct his actions and movements during his prior visit to the ladies' room. The Policeman observed him from different angles, jotted down notes, drew an extremely precise sketch, strode purposefully around the room, measuring its dimensions, and used his mobile telephone to take photographs of the broken towel dispenser, of the towel itself (which he'd extracted from the trash can after slipping on a fresh pair of surgical gloves), and of the Investigator (close-ups, frontal and profile views). He put some questions to the Investigator and ascertained that the stains on his trousers and jacket hadn't disappeared. When he finally seemed convinced that the Investigator wasn't hiding anything and had told him nothing but the truth, the Policeman asked the suspect to accompany him to his space.

"Your *space*? What space?"

"My office, if you prefer. Surely you don't think I'm going to let you go without taking a statement from you?"

"A statem—"

The Policeman was already walking away, so the Investigator was forced to follow in his footsteps. They left the restroom. The Policeman closed the door behind them and put seals on it, to the Investigator's great astonishment. Then they crossed the immense breakfast room, passed in front of the reception desk, which was still deserted, and stopped before a door situated to the right of the counter. This door bore a sign: STAFF ONLY. The Policeman drew a key from his pocket, opened the door, and showed the Investigator in.

It was a broom closet whose jumbled contents included a great many buckets, floor cloths, sponges, dustpans, and cleaning products, along with a very large vacuum cleaner. In one corner, an electric typewriter stood on a pair of boards laid across two trestles.

"I can't stand computers," said the Policeman, having noticed the Investigator's skeptical look. "Computers dehumanize relations."

He held out a pink plastic bucket to the Investigator, who took hold of it without grasping its purpose. Then the Policeman seized another bucket, a blue one, turned it upside down, and sat on it. "Go on, don't be afraid," he said. "They're pretty sturdy and quite comfortable, too, once you get used to them. My chairs haven't been delivered yet."

The Policeman inserted a sheet of paper into the typewriter. He performed this act most meticulously, removing and reinserting the sheet three times because it seemed slightly askew.

"What if I'm dealing with a madman here?" the Investigator wondered. "Maybe he's a policeman like I'm God the Father. He didn't show me his card. His office is in a hotel, and what kind of office is it? A nasty little storage room. Yes, that's it—he's nuts! Why has it taken me so long to see that?"

The thought revived his confidence. He nearly burst out laughing, but he restrained himself. Better not to let anything show, better to play along with this lunatic for a few more minutes, and then to clear out at top speed. He'd have plenty of time that evening to lodge a complaint with the

Hotel Management about this obviously sick person, who must be a deranged janitor.

"There we are!" exclaimed the Policeman, smiling broadly at the sight of the white page, perfectly horizontal and flawlessly aligned with the upper edge of the type-writer's platen.

"I'm at your service," the Investigator replied.

A BRIGHT SUN WAS BLEACHING the already very pale
sky. The temperature was mild, almost hot, totally
unlike the chill of the previous night. The Investigator blinked and stood unmoving for a moment on the Hotel
steps, incredulous, happy, and relieved to be outside at last,
however late in the day. He felt a little better. Could that be
because of the medicine the Policeman had given him?

After having been so harried and upset during the past
few hours, he was ready to become the Investigator again: a
scrupulous, professional, careful, disciplined, and methodi-
cal person who didn't allow himself to be surprised or both-
ered by the circumstances or individuals he was required to
encounter in the course of his investigations.

On the sidewalk a few yards away, a human flood—a
dense, fast-moving, utterly silent Crowd—was streaming
past him as though pulled along by a powerful force of suction. The Crowd consisted of men and women of all ages,
but they were all walking at the same speed, in silence, their
eyes fixed on the ground or staring straight ahead. Equally
strange was the fact that the Crowd on the nearer sidewalk
was moving from left to right, while the Crowd on the sidewalk across the street was moving in the opposite direction,

as though someone somewhere had instituted foot-traffic rules and no one dared go the wrong way.

The only perceptible sound, very soft, came from the vehicles on the street as they crawled along in one direction, from right to left. It was a huge traffic jam! The cars drove past extremely slowly, but in a most orderly fashion, and the Investigator was unable to detect any signs of agitation on the faces of the drivers; they kept their eyes fixed on what was in front of them and seemed to be suffering in silence. There were no horns blowing, no shouted insults—nothing but the elegant, muffled, almost inaudible hum of the engines.

The rhythm of the City had decidedly changed. Though deserted by night, by day it presented an image of great liveliness, of an industrious, concentrated, steady, fluid animation that excited the Investigator and provoked a surge of energy in him. Of course, given the empty desolation of the streets at night, the dense Crowd and heavy traffic were surprising, but when he considered the disconcerting events he'd just lived through and the weird persons he'd had to deal with, he felt he was getting back to a kind of normality. He wanted to accept it and avoid pondering hard questions.

Once again, however, the Investigator had to get his bearings. He'd chosen not to ask the Policeman for directions, being certain that the man, policeman or not, would use the request as an excuse to ask him another endless series of questions and maybe even to place him in custody in his cubbyhole.

The Investigator examined the structures he was able to see: immense warehouses, rows of large metal or stone sheds, office towers, administrative buildings, huge park-

ing garages, laboratories, metal chimneys emitting clouds of
nearly transparent smoke. The heterogeneity of those structures was in fact only superficial, for they all belonged to the
operations of the Enterprise, as was demonstrated by the wall
that encompassed them; and as the wall defined a boundary,
it also created bonds, connections, bridges, and attachments
between the entities it enclosed, absorbing them into the cells
and members of a single, individual, gigantic body.

The whole City seemed to consist of the Enterprise, as if
little by little, in a process of expansion nothing had been
able to check, the Enterprise had extended itself beyond its
original limits, swallowing up, digesting, and assimilating
the neighborhoods on its perimeter by imbuing them with
its own identity. The mysterious force emanating from the
whole caused the Investigator to suffer a brief dizzy spell.
Although he'd been aware for a long time that his place in
the world and in society was microscopic in scale, this vision
of the Enterprise, this glimpse of its brazen extent, allowed
him to discover another unsettling fact: his anonymity. Over
and above the knowledge that he wasn't anything, he suddenly realized that he wasn't anyone, either. The thought
didn't distress him, but all the same, it entered his mind as
a narrow, curious worm penetrates an already fragile fruit.

But when he spotted a recess in the wall about two hundred yards to his left, on the other side of the street, he was
strangely captivated by the sight and broke off his reverie.
Yes, that wide angle, that break in the even line of the wall—
there was no doubt about it—had to be the entrance. The
entrance to the Enterprise. The entrance where the Guardhouse was located. And to think that the Hotel was barely a
minute away. He'd needed several hours to trudge from one

to the other, and by God knew what impossible route. It was pretty laughable. The Investigator felt almost euphoric.

He went down the four steps to the sidewalk and looked for a pedestrian crossing area where he could get across the street. But it was no use. He scanned his surroundings as carefully as he could, bending down until his face was at ground level, peering past the legs of the pedestrians and under the wheels of the passing vehicles in an attempt to catch sight of the distinctive white stripes, then going back up the four steps and standing on tiptoe on the top one, trying to descry a traffic light, whether near or far, but, try as he might, he could discover no crossing anywhere.

The Investigator pondered for a few moments, told himself he'd lost enough time already, and resolved to cross the stream of vehicles. It shouldn't be much of a problem, he thought, given their greatly reduced speed.

THE INITIAL PROBLEM, whose difficulty he had in fact totally underestimated, was to get to the edge of the sidewalk, that is, to traverse the moving, compact mass of men and women who were hurrying past him. They formed a sort of border, two or three yards wide, with a dense, mobile, quietly hostile texture.

At first, the Investigator tried various forms of apology, all uttered in a loud voice and accompanied by modest gestures expressing his desire to pass. Those proved ineffective, as did all his demonstrations of the most consummate politeness; no one stopped, no one shifted position to allow him to slip between the moving bodies. The men and women walking hurriedly along didn't look at him, either. Many of them were wearing headphones or had earpieces stuck in their ears; others, also very numerous, were sending messages or receiving calls on a kind of mobile telephone with a single button, identical to the phone the Policeman carried.

The Investigator told himself that in these conditions he would have to grit his teeth and force his way through. The time had come for him to stop hesitating and start using his elbows, even if that meant stepping on a few feet or jostling some pedestrians. In any case, he'd had it with people not paying attention to him. He took a deep breath and plunged in.

It was a strange stampede. There was no aggressiveness in its forward surge—a great throng of bodies moving implacably along without outcries, without insults, without inappropriate gestures, without hatred—but it was fraught with mute, extreme, perplexing violence. The Investigator had two distinct, simultaneous impressions: that he was swimming in a torrent of tumultuous water, and that he was being pushed by a bulldozer made of some soft and yielding material. He thrashed, grabbed, scratched, seized, released, yelled, cried, apostrophized, groaned, begged, even abased himself. He exhibited an energy that he summoned up from his very depths. Finally, he reached the curb.

His effort had truly been as enormous as the distance covered was small. Out of breath, he noticed that his raincoat, which already looked like an old, badly ironed sheet, had greatly suffered in the struggle: The right pocket had been torn, and a flap of fabric was hanging down like a big dog's ear, soft and ungainly. He wasted no time bemoaning the loss, for he still had to make his way across the stream of vehicles.

The Investigator raised his hand and gestured in the direction of the first vehicle to his left, signaling to the driver that he was going to cross the street, but he hadn't gone more than two or three steps, just enough to get past the first car and prepare to slip between the next two, when innumerable automobile horns started blowing all at once, setting up a racket that petrified him.

The noise was so outrageously loud that he wondered whether it could actually be real. He reopened his eyes—he'd shut them, as if reflexively, a few seconds earlier—and saw that all the vehicles had stopped moving. In each of them, the driver, whether a man or a woman, was sounding the horn most ferociously, and worst of all, worst of all, every one of those drivers, dozens, hundreds of drivers, was looking at him, the Investigator, frozen in place among the vehicles.

Cold sweat ran down the nape of his neck. All at once, the horns stopped. But immediately, the sound of thousands of voices—mingled, concurrent, united—rose from the sidewalks in a phenomenal hubbub. It was as if all the spectators in a stadium had started shouting at the same time. And as with the vehicles, all the men and women on the sidewalks, people who a few moments ago had been hurrying along in order and silence, maintaining an even, regular pace, absorbed in their own thoughts, their own music, their telephone conversations, and not in the least concerned with their surroundings—they had all stopped short, and they were all looking at him and shouting inaudible words in his direction, inaudible because they collided with, smashed against, shattered upon one another, distorted by the ricochets of their ground-up syllables. He panicked, tottered, barely caught himself by leaning on the hood of a car, and then turned back and stepped up onto the sidewalk he'd stepped off of less than a minute before.

He was trembling. All interest in him had ceased. On the street, the vehicles were slowly streaming past, their drivers' eyes staring straight ahead. Similarly, on both sidewalks, people had begun to walk again. Order had retuned everywhere. But what kind of order?

Imperceptibly, the Crowd caught him up in its movement. There was no resisting it. Even before his brain could decide, his legs had adopted the rhythm of the other legs around them. Now he was walking, too, and in the direction dictated by the Crowd, even though that direction was wrong, since it took him off to the right, whereas the entrance to the Enterprise, the Guardhouse, was over there, a few hundred yards away, on the left.

XIV

HIS EXPERIENCES WHILE HE WAS involuntarily adrift in the Crowd were without a doubt the strangest he'd gone through since his arrival in the City. When he allowed himself to be carried away like a wisp of straw on the current of a mighty river, the Investigator surrendered. For the first time in his existence, he gave up thinking of himself as an individual with a free will and freedom of choice, residing in a country that guaranteed fundamental human rights, so fundamental that most of the time its citizens, including the Investigator, enjoyed those rights without being fully conscious of them. Dissolved in the immense, moving mass of silent pedestrians, he slid along, stopped thinking, refused to analyze the situation, made no effort to fight it. It was almost as though he'd abandoned his body in order to enter into another body, vast and limitless.

How long did it all last? Who could really know? Not the Investigator, in any case, and that was for sure. He no longer knew very much. Like a man afflicted by a powerful psychotropic drug, he'd forgotten his raison d'être. He continued to exist, but weakly. He was losing thickness.

It started to get cooler again, and then it abruptly became cold. The sky was covered with a gray veil from which a few snowflakes soon escaped. Two or three of them, little, icy, ephemeral points, fell on the Investigator's head and brought him back to his present condition. Shivering, he realized that a sign was becoming visible up ahead in the distance, above the flowing masses of people and vehicles: a hotel sign, *his* Hotel's sign, the sign for the Hope Hotel. He told himself it had come to this: His perceptions were obviously in total disarray. He'd thought the Crowd had been sweeping him along for hours, but in fact he hadn't gone very far at all.

All the same, one detail gave him pause. Was that really the same Hotel? The same sign? Something had changed. The Hotel was in its place on the other side of the street, between two buildings he also positively recognized. On the other side of the street. On the other si—! But of course! That was what was different. If the Hotel was on the other side of the street, that meant he couldn't be on that side anymore, which therefore meant that he'd crossed over at some point, and that he was now walking on the side where the entrance to the Enterprise was located! And, yes, there, there it was, on his left, a little farther on, that was the entrance! He could even make out the Guardhouse.

He had to move fast. He had only a few seconds to get as far to the left as he could, slipping sideways across the current of humanity, so that he might escape from the streaming Crowd, leave the mass, and become again a discrete, unique creature. Just a few steps more, a few more yards, he didn't want to time his exit wrong, he didn't want to be blocked at the last moment by somebody he hadn't seen closing up behind him. . . .

Phew! Made it!

XV

B Y DAY, THE GUARDHOUSE LOOKED much less hostile than
it did at night. After all, it was just an ordinary building, simple, graceless, almost ugly, and there was nothing military about it. The Investigator didn't have to buzz
the intercom to get a response. By stepping up close to the
window and bending forward a little toward the twenty or so
concentrically arranged holes that pierced it, he was able to
address the Guard—a man neither young nor old, with a full
face and thinning hair, dressed in white like a Lab Assistant
or a Chemist—who was sitting on the other side of the glass
barrier, smiling and waiting.

"Good morning!" said the Investigator, sensing that he
was finally going to talk to someone attentive.

"Good morning," the Guard replied affably.

"I'm the Investigator."

The Guard didn't lose his smile, but the Investigator
noticed that his eyes had changed. The Guard looked him
over. This examination lasted several seconds, at the end of
which the Guard consulted a large register that lay open in
front of him. Apparently failing to find what he was looking
for, he checked the preceding pages, shifting his gaze from
line to line with the help of his right index finger. Eventu-

ally, he stopped at one of the lines and tapped it three times. "Your arrival was scheduled for yesterday at five p.m."

"Indeed," replied the Investigator, "but I was considerably delayed."

"May I see some identification, please?" the Guard asked.

"Of course!" The Investigator thrust his hand into his inside jacket pocket, found nothing, rummaged in his other pockets, began to grow pale, patted his raincoat, and then suddenly remembered that he'd given his identity papers as well as his credit card to the Giantess, who had deposited them in the Hotel safe while he looked on. On leaving the Hotel that morning, he'd completely forgotten to ask for them back. "I'm very sorry," he said, "but I've left everything at my Hotel. The Hope Hotel, you must know it, it's only a few hundred yards from here. On the other side of the street."

These words caused a darkening of the Guard's heretofore pleasant expression. He seemed to reflect for a while. The Investigator tried to maintain his own broad smile, as if doing so would convince the other of his honesty.

"Please give me a few seconds," the Guard said. He closed the register, switched off the microphone that linked him to the exterior, picked up a telephone, and dialed a number. His call must have been answered pretty quickly, because the Investigator could see him talking. The conversation went on and on. The Guard opened the register again, placed his finger on the line where the time of the Investigator's arrival was recorded, engaged in a lengthy discussion, appeared to reply to numerous questions, scrutinized the Investigator carefully, and then, finally, hung up and switched the microphone back on. "Someone will come for you," he said. "You can wait in front of the security barrier on your right."

The Investigator thanked the Guard and directed his steps to the indicated area.

The chevaux-de-frise, the rolls of barbed wire, the portcullises, and the chicanes had all been removed. Only a large, automated metal barrier blocked the entrance of the Enterprise. A Security Officer stood near the barrier. He was wearing a gray paramilitary uniform and a peaked cap of the same color, and numerous objects hung from the broad belt that girded his waist: a nightstick, a paralyzing-gas grenade, an electric pistol, a pair of handcuffs, a bunch of keys, a portable telephone, a pocket flashlight, a knife in its sheath, and a walkie-talkie. His other equipment included an earphone and a little microphone attached to the lapel of his military jacket.

When he saw the Investigator approaching the barrier, the Security Officer moved from his position and took a few slow steps forward to block the newcomer's passage, but the earphone and little microphone started sizzling at once. The Security Officer stopped, froze, listened to what he was being told, and replied simply: "Got it."

The Security Officer, who stood two heads taller than the Investigator, gazed absently at the distant roofs and ignored him. Once again, the Investigator felt uneasy. "Really, what must I look like?" he wondered. He was unshaven; he had a sizable swollen wound on his forehead; his nose was raw and running nonstop; the torn pocket of his thoroughly wrinkled raincoat was hanging down like a flap; his shoes, still wet, resembled small wads of badly tanned animal skin; and no matter how much he tugged at the lapels of his raincoat, his efforts to conceal the two big coffee stains on his jacket and trousers were in vain.

[✲]

"A bum, that's what," he thought, answering his own question. "Maybe even a drunk—me, a drunk, when I hardly ever touch alcohol." The Security Officer's outfit, by contrast, was impeccable: no wrinkles, no stains, no torn fabric. His perfectly polished boots mocked the snowflakes that fell on them. His face was closely shaven. Everything about him was clean and new, as though he'd just come out of a box.

"What weather!" the Investigator said with a little smile, but the Security Officer made no reply. This didn't so much offend the Investigator as hurt his feelings. Did he count for so little? Was he so utterly insignificant? The effects of the two tablets he'd washed down with the awful coffee were fading. A great weariness invaded his whole body, while at the same time each of his bones became a focal point of pain. His head was caught in a vise, and the jaws of the vise, cranked tighter and tighter by a pitiless hand, were gradually crushing his temples. He was hot. He was cold. He shivered, sweated, sneezed, coughed, choked, and coughed again.

"Keep your germs to yourself, we really don't need them right now!"

XVI

THOROUGHLY OCCUPIED IN SNEEZING, he hadn't heard the approach of the man who'd just addressed him so peremptorily.

"Are you the Investigator?"

The Investigator nodded almost reluctantly, blowing his nose at the same time.

"I'm the Guide. I'll be escorting you to the Manager's office. Don't be offended if I don't shake your hand. Here, this is for you."

The Guide looked as though he might be the Investigator's age. Of about middle height, with a slightly fleshy face and not much hair, he was wearing an elegant gray suit. He handed the Investigator a bag in which the latter found various objects: a long white coat, a hard hat of the same color, a pen, a key ring adorned with a photograph of an old man with a mustache—the same man whose framed photograph hung on the wall of his Hotel room?—a notebook and a little plastic flag, both bearing the logo of the Enterprise, and a badge with the words "External Element" printed in bold type.

"It's the traditional welcome gift. I'll ask you to put on the coat immediately, clip your badge to the upper left pocket, and place the hard hat on your head."

"Of course," said the Investigator, as if he found these instructions completely natural. The long white coat was several sizes too big and the hat too small. As for the badge, it was perfect.

"Will you please follow me?"

The Investigator needed no second invitation. Things were finally starting to get serious. He was glad to have the coat on, big as it was, because it hid the state his own clothes were in; furthermore, the hard hat offered his skull a little gentle warmth, as if a beloved hand were caressing his head, and sheltered him from the snow, which was falling more and more thickly. His strength was returning.

"You don't wear anything?" the Investigator asked.

"I beg your pardon?"

"A hard hat, a white coat. You don't wear anything like that?"

"No. They're useless, to tell you the truth, but absolutely obligatory for External Elements. We always observe the rules. Please take care not to drift away from the line!"

As they walked, they followed a red line painted on the ground. Parallel to the red line were three others: a yellow line, a green line, and a blue line. The Investigator took advantage of this opportunity to ask the Guide exactly what activities the Enterprise was engaged in. "That's a vast question," the Guide began, "and I'm not the person best qualified to respond to it. I don't know everything. Actually, I don't know very much. The Enterprise is active in so many areas: communications, engineering, water treatment, renewable energy, nuclear chemistry, oil and gas production, stock analysis, pharmaceutical research, nanotechnology, gene therapy, food processing, banking, insurance, mining, concrete, real estate, storage and consolidation of nonconventional data resources, armaments, humanitarian development, micro-credit aid programs, education and training, textiles, plastics, publishing, public works, patrimony preservation, investment and tax counseling, agriculture, logging, mental analysis, entertainment, surgery, aid to disaster victims, and obviously other fields I'm forgetting! In fact, I'm not sure there's any sector of human activity that doesn't depend directly or indirectly on the Enterprise or one of its subsidiaries. Well, we're almost there."

The Investigator was having trouble digesting the list the Guide had just enumerated. He'd been far from suspecting that the Enterprise covered all those areas; it was difficult for him to understand how such a range could be possible. The fleeting sensation that he was going alone to face a body with a thousand heads panicked him.

The two men were approaching a cone-shaped glass building. The Investigator noticed that the yellow, green, and blue lines turned right, but the red line ended at the conical building's entrance.

"Kindly step in." The Guide held the door open for him, and they both went inside. A circular stairway turned round upon itself as it rose to the upper floors; it was a little like the staircase in the Hope Hotel, but here the risers all appeared to be of equal height. Behind frosted-glass doors, the visitor could make out unmoving silhouettes, persons of indeterminate sex who seemed to be seated at desks in front of parallelepiped shapes that might have been computers. The atmosphere was very silent, almost reverential.

"Would you mind waiting a few moments while I inform the Manager that you're here? In the meantime, please have a seat." The Guide indicated three chairs arranged around a low table on which lay a certain number of what looked like brochures. "I've asked a Colleague to put together a collection of documents for your perusal. They'll give you an idea of the Enterprise's social policy, of how the Enterprise works, and of the Enterprise's unwavering concern for its employees' well-being."

The Investigator thanked the Guide, who then began to climb the stairs. His footfalls resounded as though he were treading on the stone floor of a cathedral. As he progressed, his body dwindled but remained visible, thanks to the transparent steps of azure-hued glass that mounted skyward up the giant spiral.

The chair the Investigator had chosen quickly proved uncomfortable. Because the seat was inclined slightly forward, he couldn't stop sliding on it. He started to change chairs but ascertained that the other two presented the same defect. Tightening his thigh muscles, he tried to forget his discomfort by plunging into the leaflets and booklets that lay on the table.

They formed a veritable miscellany: Some press clippings about the Enterprise mingled with the menus offered at the cafeteria during the last two months of the preceding year; an organizational chart rendered absolutely illegible by the low quality of the photocopy was paired with a report on a visit to an Asian industrialist specializing in the manufacture of soy sauce. A smallish bound volume purported to set out, according to its title, a complete list of the personnel active in the Enterprise as of January 1 of the current year, but this book contained nothing but two or three hundred blank pages. The Investigator also came upon some application forms for a tango evening organized by the Region 3 Transport Service Technical Executives' Association, a circular informing the warehousemen in the International Packaging Sector about the opening of a rest home located in the Balkans, a user's manual in ten languages for a dictating machine with a German brand name, an invoice for the purchase of thirty liters of liquid soap, and some twenty photographs of a place under construction whose location and purpose weren't specified.

The Investigator perused each of these documents conscientiously, telling himself he might thus come to understand by what logic they had been assembled, but that mystery remained completely opaque. Nonetheless, he needed half an hour to read all the words and contemplate all the images presented in the collection, and when he was finished, the Guide had still not come back downstairs.

The Investigator suddenly clapped his hand to his stomach. A long, gurgling rumble had just shaken his innards. Not surprising. Nothing had gone down his throat since the two heinous rusks he'd consumed that morning, and the previous evening, he hadn't eaten anything at all. Some distance away, behind the first curve of the stairway, he saw what looked like a vending machine. He had two coins left. Could he perhaps find something over there to calm his hunger? He stood up and discovered that because of those blasted chairs, his muscles were totally cramped.

Hobbling, bent in half, his thighs hard and tense, he headed for the vending machine. The skirts of his coat trailed the floor, and he tripped on them twice, almost falling both times, but the sight of the display behind the machine's glass front sufficed to make him forget his pains. There was a large selection of cold and hot drinks, but, more important—and this he hadn't expected at all—there were dozens of sandwiches, chicken, ham, sausage, tuna, all garnished with green lettuce leaves, sliced tomatoes, and mayonnaise, all magnificently fresh in appearance, each neatly wrapped in cellophane and waiting in the refrigerated interior.

XVII

H E SELECTED A CUP OF HOT CHOCOLATE and a "Peasant"
sandwich, whose descriptive label proposed "a generous
helping of ham, cured in traditional style and carved
off the bone, served between two slices of whole-grain bread
dressed with lightly salted butter, mixed lettuce leaves, pick-
led gherkins, and thinly sliced tomatoes."

Number 7 for the chocolate and number 32 for the Peasant. The Investigator inserted his coins, punched in the numbers, and pressed the "Order" key, which began to blink. The
machine spoke to him: "Your order is being processed. Number 7. Hot chocolate. If you want more sugar, press 'Sugar.'"

It was a synthetic voice, mechanical, vaguely feminine,
agreeable to the ear in spite of a strong foreign accent of
indefinable origin. The machine made various sounds—of
liquid being drawn up, of valves opening and closing, of
suction and expulsion—and then, on the right, a little door
slid open, revealing the spout of a kind of percolator. Steam
came out of this spout, soon followed by a smooth jet of scalding hot, deliciously fragrant, rich, creamy chocolate, which
streamed down before the Investigator's eyes as he stared
at it in dismay, for no plastic cup had appeared to catch the

liquid. When the stream came to an end, the artificial voice expressed the wish that the Investigator would enjoy his beverage, and it was only after the machine fell silent again that the plastic cup, with a distinct, ironic "plop," dropped into position to receive the lost drink. The Investigator, however, had no time for either irritation or despair; sandwich number 32 was on its way.

"You ordered a Peasant sandwich. Please collect it from the delivery box at the bottom front of the dispenser. We hope you enjoy your meal."

The rotating display rack that held the sandwiches went into motion. It pivoted three times in such a way as to place number 32 in front of a remote-controlled arm, which seized it, removed it from its compartment, and carried it about twelve inches through the air. Then the four pincers at the end of the arm opened and released the Peasant. It fell toward the delivery box, but about eight inches before reaching its goal, it got caught on the tray that featured the number 65 sandwich, the "Ocean": "A thick, tasty slice of red tuna on a round roll, enhanced with sesame seeds, olive oil, curly endive, onions, and capers."

The Investigator struck the glass front of the vending machine a few sharp blows with the flat of his hand, but to no avail; the Peasant would not leave the Oceans. He struck the machine harder and harder, took hold of it with both hands, and shook it in every direction, but the only result he obtained was to make the synthetic voice repeat its message, congratulating him on his choice, reminding him that he was about to savor a meal prepared according to the strictest sanitary and dietary norms and in conformity with international Conventions, and wishing him an enjoyable dining experience.

He threw himself to his knees, thrust his arm into the delivery box, twisted his body, shoved his hard hat, which was hindering his movements, high up on his head, and stretched out his hand and his fingers as far as he could, but, alas, despite all his efforts, his impotent middle finger remained a good four inches from the sandwich.

"You should have asked me!"

The Investigator hurriedly yanked his arm out of the machine, like a thief surprised by the police with his hand in an old lady's purse.

The Guide looked at him and shook his head. "I would have told you it doesn't work. We've called the manufacturer I don't know how many times, but we can't make ourselves understood. They've outsourced their production unit to Bangladesh, and we don't yet have anyone on the staff who speaks Bengali. It's not a problem to reach them by telephone, but then communication turns out to be impossible. Don't look at me like that—you're not the first victim, we've all been had by this machine. Such a shame, because when it works it's really a very good thing. Shall we go? The Manager's expecting you."

The Guide was already walking toward the stairway. The Investigator got to his feet as quickly as he could, pulled his coat straight, repositioned his hard hat, which was on the point of falling, and followed him. The gurgling in his belly was getting louder. He absolutely had to eat something; if he didn't, he was sincerely afraid he might faint. The beginning of the climb up the stairs was quite difficult, because his feet kept getting tangled up in his coat. He was forced to grab its skirts with both hands and raise them about eight inches or so, like a bride lifting the tulle cascades of her long-trained gown. He felt totally ridiculous.

"Did you have time to take a look at the informational materials?" the Guide asked.

With a gesture, the Investigator indicated that he had.

"Very instructive, don't you think? I'm not the person who prepared the dossier for you—I merely supervised the project. I've been assigned a Colleague from our Temporary Processing branch, which has undergone a reduction in personnel. He was the one who did the job. It's too bad he can't stay with me, but he's being sent to the Conceptualization Department. A peerless Co-Worker, brilliant, subtle, involved, with a remarkable capacity for synthesizing data; a man utterly representative of the culture of the Enterprise. We need more like him."

The Investigator thought the best course would be not to reply. Reply to what? In all probability, he and the Guide hadn't read the same documents; the ones the Guide was talking about must have been switched with those he'd been given, which must previously have been destined for the rubbish bin or the paper shredder.

The helicoid formed by the stairway was excessively harmonious. Though probably useless in terms of efficiency, it gave the person mounting the stairs a rare sensation of light, unencumbered ascent into a space where breaks, angles, and whatever might be pointed, aggressive, or wounding were unknown. The higher he climbed, the closer he got to the central axis, because the distance between it and the stairs steadily diminished, so that in the end the Investigator had the impression that he was turning round and round upon himself without rising any higher, which reinforced his vertigo and made him, for a time, forget his hunger.

"Here we are," said the Guide.

The two of them were standing in front of a large door made of precious wood. No handle or doorknob was visible.

"Go ahead and knock, the Manager knows you're coming. As for me, my mission ends here. I don't think we'll see each other again, so please accept my best wishes for the rest of your day. I won't shake your hand."

The Guide made a bow to the Investigator, who felt obliged to return the bow, lest he seem impolite. The Guide walked away down a narrow corridor and, after a few seconds, disappeared around a bend.

The Investigator checked to make sure his coat was correctly buttoned and his badge properly straight. He readjusted his hard hat, which still had a tendency to slip, and then he knocked on the door: three quick raps. As if by magic, in the most perfect silence, the portal opened. He was greeted by a violently bright light, perhaps a projector, focused on him and blinding him. He blinked and shielded his eyes with his right hand, and then he heard a powerful voice call out, "Come in! Come on in! Enter! Come right in, please! Don't be afraid!"

XVIII

ONCE AGAIN, ONE MORE TIME, the Investigator thought about death. Hadn't he read—he couldn't remember where—some stories about experiences on the outer limits, about certain people who'd returned from the frontiers of the hereafter? And didn't they describe an intense, irradiant light and a sort of large tunnel they'd moved through before turning back? The glass cone he'd entered, the strange staircase winding around upon itself, the bright sun pouring each of its dazzling particles of light into his eyes and drowning them, weren't all those things variations of the big tunnel?

"Please don't stop so far away! Please, I beg you! Come closer! Do come closer!"

The voice was strong and a little wry. The Investigator reflected that God, if He existed, surely didn't have a voice like that; it sounded more like a used-car salesman's voice, or a politician's.

"What are you doing with that hard hat on your head? My poor friend! Who told you to wear that grotesque thing? You're not in a shipyard! Come closer to me! Come on!"

No, decidedly, this couldn't be God. God wouldn't have made that remark about hard hats in a shipyard. And if this wasn't God, then he, the Investigator, wasn't dead, and furthermore, the light was nothing but a very bright light with nothing divine about it. But why in the world was it still aimed straight at him? He said, "The problem is, I can't see anything. . . ."

"What do you mean, you can't see anything? I can see you perfectly well! Perfectly!"

"It's blinding me," the Investigator groaned.

"Blinding you? Good heavens!" the voice replied. "Of course, of course! Who the devil installed this bloody . . . Wait a moment!"

The Investigator heard a small, sharp sound, and then he was plunged in total darkness.

"Is that better?" asked the voice.

"I can't see anything now, not a thing," the Investigator complained.

"It's not possible! I can still see *you*! This is crazy! Shut your eyes for a few seconds, then reopen them slowly, and I'm convinced you'll see me! Go on! Trust me! Shut your eyes, I tell you!"

The Investigator resigned himself to obeying. He didn't have much to lose. After all, if he was dead, he couldn't be deader, he thought, since death is a state that does not admit gradations. You can't be very dead or exceptionally dead. You're just dead, period.

He reopened his eyes and discovered the room he'd just entered. It put him in mind of a film producer's office. He'd never seen one in his life, but he had an idea of such a room that was at once quite accurate and entirely imaginary: the scent of essential oils, shelves displaying trophies and awards, a bar cart, a humidor, a plush carpet, leather armchairs, a desk with a broad rosewood top; on it a paper cutter, a luxury pen, a desk blotter, a pencil cup, a letter box. On the wall there was an immense portrait of an old man who looked to the Investigator like the man on the key ring.

"All right, can you see me now?"

The Investigator nodded, but in fact he could make out only a thick, blurry form half seated on the left side of the desk.

"But, good Lord, will you please take off that hard hat! Who decked you out in a hard hat?"

"They told me it was obligatory."

"Obligatory! Who's 'they'? There's no 'they' here. I want a name. Who was it? And this coat? I have to admire your docility!"

"I'd prefer to keep the coat on, if you don't mind," the Investigator said quickly. He didn't want to get the Guide in trouble about the hard hat, and he was mindful of the deplorable condition of the clothes he was wearing under the coat.

"As you wish! Come closer and have a seat."

The Investigator took off the hard hat and approached the desk. The blurred form rose and became clearer, revealing a man of less than average height and well-advanced baldness. His roundish features were barely illuminated by a light that came from the ceiling, like a rain of golden particles.

"Sit down, sit down. . . ."

The man indicated one of the two armchairs, and the Investigator sat down. He felt so utterly lost in the chair, which was of an unusual size, that he had the sensation of having shrunk. He arranged the bottom of the coat in such a way as to hide his trousers and placed the hard hat in his lap.

"Before we start," said the man, who the Investigator thought must be the Manager the Guide had mentioned, "what I want is for you to make yourself perfectly comfortable. I want you to feel at home. I want you to feel exactly as if you were at home. Is everything all right?"

"Everything's fine."

"Did you say something just now about being blinded?"

"That was because of your light, I couldn't see anything. It was a figure of speech. An image."

The Manager clapped his hands together and stood up. "Watch out, you're talking to me about images, and I don't want images, I want facts, I want clear-sightedness. I'm counting on you a great deal, and when I say 'I,' I mean 'we.' You understand?"

"Of course," replied the Investigator, who didn't understand very much, and who moreover had the impression that he was slowly being digested by the armchair.

"Very good, then! Are you feeling well? You look pretty pale. . . ."

The Investigator hesitated, but then, since he was feeling weaker by the minute, he went against his true nature and took the plunge: "To tell you the truth, I'm just about starving. If it might be possible to eat something . . ."

"Possible? You must be jesting! Of course it's possible! Must I remind you who you are? Aren't you . . ." The Manager hesitated, rummaged in his pockets, and pulled out a pack of index cards, which he rapidly consulted. "Aren't you . . . let's see . . . you're . . . you are . . . Ah, my goodness, where have I put your card?!"

"I'm the Investigator."

"There you go. Exactly! You're the Investigator! Are you really the Investigator?"

"Yes."

"Can you possibly think that, in an enterprise such as ours, we're not going to do all we can to make sure your Investigation is conducted under the most favorable conditions?"

"Indeed, that would be very kind of you. . . ."

"Well, then!" And he started laughing as he picked up his telephone. "This is the Manager speaking. Bring us something for the Investigator to eat. As soon as possible."

He fell silent, seemed to be listening attentively to what was being said at the other end of the line, shook his head several times, covered the mouthpiece with his hand, and addressed the Investigator: "Chicken-liver salad, roast beef, green beans, goat cheese, chocolate fondant. It's nothing much, and I apologize, but would that be all right?"

"But that's . . . that's wonderful," the Investigator managed to stammer, barely able to believe his ears.

"And to drink? Red wine, white wine, beer, raki, ouzo, grappa, pisco, Tokay, cognac, aquavit, bourbon; mineral water: sparkling or still, and from where? Fiji? Iceland? Italy? Guatemala?"

"Perhaps something warm," the Investigator ventured to say, since he was shivering from cold. "Some tea, preferably . . ."

"Tea? Japanese, Taiwanese, Russian, Ceylon, Darjeeling, white, black, green, red, blue?"

"I'll have, uh . . . regular tea," the Investigator ventured.

"Regular? No problem!" replied the Manager, repeated the order, and hung up. "And there we are!" he said. "You see, you were right to speak up! The Enterprise's kitchens, like the Enterprise itself, never stop. They work at all hours of the day and night, every day of the year."

"But . . . is it still day?" the Investigator asked doubtfully.

"Of course it's still day! Look at that light," the Manager said, pointing at the big bay windows. "Now, for the sake of honesty, I must tell you that the beef comes from the Southern Hemisphere. Do you have any objection to that?"

"What beef?"

"The beef for the roast, the dish I just ordered for you!"

The Investigator smiled slightly.

"Good," the Manager declared. "Now all we have to do is wait."

He folded his arms across his abdomen and gave the Investigator a kindly look. The Investigator replied with a rather forced smile and sank a bit more deeply into his armchair. His head was now only a little higher than the armrests. The Manager sighed, and the two of them waited.

XIX

A S IT HAPPENED, THEY WAITED a long time. After a while, finding that silence and smiles had their limits, the Manager—who was sitting beside the Investigator, in the other armchair—initiated a conversation by assuring his guest that his meal would arrive momentarily. Then he said, "We're going through some difficult times, as you surely know. Who can tell what the future holds for us, for you, me, the planet? Nothing's simple. Care for some water? No? As you wish. After all—if you'll allow me, I believe I can confide in you—a person in my position is very much alone, terribly alone, and you're some kind of doctor, aren't you?"

"Not really . . ." the Investigator murmured.

"Come, don't be so modest!" said the Manager, tapping his visitor on the thigh. Then he took a long, deep breath, shut his eyes, exhaled, and opened his eyes again. "Remind me, what's the exact purpose of your visit?"

"To tell the truth, it's not really a visit. I'm here to conduct an Investigation into the suicides that have plagued the Enterprise."

"Suicides? News to me . . . I've been kept out of the loop, no doubt. My Co-Workers know it's best not to cross me.

Suicides, imagine that! If I'd been aware of them, God only knows what I might have done! Suicides . . ."

There was a pause, and then the Manager began to speak again in a kind of reverie. A discreet smile brightened his face, as if he were mentally caressing a pleasant idea. "Suicide. I've never thought about it, but after all, yes, why not, it's no stupider than anything else. . . ."

When he went on after the next pause, the smile had been left behind. "You know, I devote my time to one thing only: trying to understand why we've reached this point. I imagine that's what people expect of me, but I'm not making any progress. Results are nil. Counterproductivity, total. Is there someone somewhere, just one person, able to understand? What might your personal thoughts on this be?"

The Investigator was quite vexed by the direction the interview had taken so far. He slowly shrugged his shoulders, which could be interpreted either as concurrence with the Manager's questions or as metaphysical hesitation.

"Just so," said the Manager. "Just so. You're wise, you're maturing at a tremendous rate! But as for me, I'm not you, alas, I'm not you, I've got my hands in the grease. I'm just a simple pawn, a sort of flour mite. Have you read the philosophers? Of course you've read them, a man like you has read them. Believe it or not, they send me into a state of intellectual catalepsy. It's drastic. And they must know it, the bastards! Without a doubt, they did it on purpose. Basically, they were exceedingly cruel individuals and also incredible cowards."

As the Manager talked, he wrung his fingers as though he wanted to yank them off. "My goodness, if you knew what my days were like. Since it's just the two of us, I could tell you about them, my days, how I spend them—I spend them wondering. Yes. I wonder, I ponder. I don't leave this office. That's all I do. Under the eyes of . . ."

He broke off, coughing, and the Investigator had the impression that he was turning toward the large photograph of the good-natured, smiling old man, whose bushy white eyebrows elegantly matched the big, slightly floppy bow tie that closed his shirt collar. The Manager nodded and turned back to the Investigator.

"Yes, I wonder," the Manager began again. "What's become of our ideals? We've trampled on them, we've laid them waste! I don't mean you, I wouldn't take such a liberty, you're different, you're above, but me, me, I'm as contempt-ible as rat droppings, I'm a centipede, an old cigarette butt, wet, torn, crushed under the heel of an anonymous and scornful shoe, yes I am, yes I am, don't say no to make me feel better! I beg you, don't handle me with care! You must be terrible—just, but terrible! And all that, for what? Why? I'm asking you, I'm asking you, I know you know, because you, you do know, don't you? Don't you know?"

The Investigator, not daring to disappoint the Manager, nodded his head.

"Of course you know. . . . Oh, this is all so . . . But I'm wandering!"

He clapped his hands, sprang up nimbly, danced a few steps, caught one foot in the thick rug, and almost fell. "Look at me!" he cried. "I have resources, don't I? I'm not on my way out, not yet, despite my age! What do you think?"

The Investigator was getting weaker. His armchair had

turned into a great mouth that was gradually swallowing him, and he found the man before him, who was jumping around like an athlete warming up, even more disturbing than the Policeman in the Hotel.

The Manager began to do entrechats, up-and-down bounces, long leaps. He pirouetted and ran to the back of the room, where he made the sign of the cross, took a run-up, and charged at his desk, over which he attempted to jump and which he nearly managed to clear, except that at the last moment, when he was suspended in the air, his left foot struck the massive black marble inkwell and he crashed heavily against the glass wall.

The Investigator prepared to go to his aid, but the Manager was already getting to his feet. Smiling, he massaged a knee and an elbow, repeating the whole while, "I didn't hurt myself, not at all. I've got the hang of it. The hang of it . . . You'll tell them, won't you? You'll tell them that I'm at the peak of my powers? That I can still, I don't know what, I guess, hold on, hold on, yes, that's it, I can still hold on!!! I'm here. I'm here! You'll tell them? Please? Please . . ."

The Manager knelt before the Investigator. He lifted up his joined hands. His eyes were wet with tears. He besought his companion.

"Of course," the Investigator said, "I'll tell them. I'll tell them, there's no need to worry about that." And at the very moment when he pronounced those words, which seemed to come from someone other than himself, he wondered how he could get out of the situation he was in.

"Sometimes at night, I have the feeling that I'm the captain of an enormous airliner." The Manager's voice had thinned to a murmur. "Five hundred passengers are in my charge, or five thousand, or five hundred thousand, I don't know anymore. I'm flying the aircraft. . . ."

Still on his knees, he embraced the Investigator's legs. For several seconds, contorting his mouth, he imitated the sound of the jet engines.

"I'm the great pilot. The people in the plane sleep, read, dream about those they love, build their futures on sweet, tender fantasies, and I, I, I'm the last and only, God has placed His index finger on my forehead, I know the route, I know the skies, the stars, wind currents, souls, there's this big instrument panel in front of me, all illuminated, with all these magnificent buttons, white, opal, yellow, red, silver, all these lives that come on, go off, blink, these levers, so pleasant to the touch, how intoxicating it is to feel the destinies of all those people at my back, shut up in the same aluminum cabin, but I'm only a man, a man, damn it, why me? Why on earth am I the captain? Why me? I don't know a thing about flying! Not a thing! I don't know how to read a map, I have no sense of direction, and I've never been able to make so much as a kite take off! It's a horrible dream."

There was a silence. The Manager had begun to weep, and his tears were wetting the Investigator's trousers. Although he was thoroughly annoyed by this turn of events, the Investigator didn't dare say anything. He was pondering what to do when the Manager bounded to his feet, smoothed his pants, rubbed his face with his hands, wiped away his tears, and offered the Investigator a countenance smoothed by a beaming smile. "All the same, life is marvelous, don't you think?"

The Investigator didn't reply. He'd just seen a man in

ruins before his eyes, a man like an old, worn-out battery, unable to hold a charge, and then, suddenly, the same man— but was he truly the same?—was wiping all the tears from his face with the back of his hand and rejoicing in existence. The Investigator didn't have time to reply.

"With your permission, I need to step away for a few seconds. I'll be right back." The Manager pointed at a door located to the left of his huge desk.

"Please, go right ahead," said the Investigator. The Manager clapped his hands, performed an elegant entrechat, and danced toward the door in bossa-nova rhythm. Then, having reached his goal, he turned around, saluted an imaginary public with a graceful movement of his hand, opened the door, and vanished, closing it behind him.

XX

H UNGER IS A STRANGE CONTINENT. Up until then, the
Investigator had never imagined it as a landscape, but
he'd started to perceive its immense, desolate expanse.
He felt his head buzzing, and it seemed to him that the walls
of the room were swaying a bit. The beneficial effects of the
two tablets the Policeman had given him had long since
disappeared. He was obliged to yield to the evidence: He had
a raging fever. In spite of the overheated office and the heavy
coat keeping him warm, he was shivering. His mouth was
dry, and he had the disagreeable sensation that his tongue
was going to adhere permanently to his palate. His empty
stomach was making bizarre noises that sounded like groans,
echoes of distant quarrels, muffled shocks, minor explosions.
His vision clouded every now and then. His heart beat in
an unusual way, alternating abrupt accelerations with scary
pauses. He tried to gain a little assurance by telling himself
that the Manager had no doubt gone to inquire about the
food he'd ordered for him, and that in a few minutes he'd
come back, bringing a tray laden with the promised meal,
and all the Investigator's discomfort would cease.

The Manager . . . Was this City inhabited solely by
strange creatures like the Giantess and certifiably insane

people like the Policeman and the Manager? The latter's obscure lamentations had quite amazed the Investigator, and though he was by no means completely stupid, he hadn't understood very clearly the nature of the man's complaints. Where had he sprung from, this Manager, and why did he have this need to pour out his heart to the first stranger who came along? They weren't friends, they hardly knew each other at all! Didn't he have any self-control, any sense of propriety? How could this depressive man have been given such an important post, when you didn't have to be a psychologist to consider the evidence and conclude that he had neither the mental qualities nor the solid nerves required to discharge such a responsibility? And then there was the gigantic portrait, the photograph the Manager had gazed upon several times with mingled fear and admiration, as if he might find support there, or increased authority. Who could the subject of the portrait be, that his mere image had the power to provoke moments of veneration or dread?

The Investigator examined the picture more attentively. The old man's smile was direct, frank, and penetrating. It wasn't fake; it was the smile of a man who loved his neighbor, who knew him and looked upon him with benevolence and humanity. The old fellow was wearing a suit of elegant cut, which, though perhaps a bit outmoded, nonetheless perfectly became him, a suit made of a soft, warm, reassuring fabric, doubtless some kind of tweed. He leaned forward, as if he wished to come as close as possible to the person looking at him.

This must be the Founder, the Investigator said to himself. The Founder of the Enterprise. Who else could he be? Then again, the Investigator had no memory whatsoever of the Enterprise's having had a Founder. To be sure, it must have been founded at some point in the past, and no doubt by a particular individual. The meager documentation the Investigator had received from his Head of Section when he was charged with the Investigation provided only the tally of recorded suicides and barely mentioned the Enterprise, and the incoherent dossier the Guide had given him earlier that afternoon likewise shed no light on the subject.

Ordinarily, the Investigator did not concern himself with the origins of enterprises or look into their civil status. That wasn't his business. Moreover, in the world where he lived, such origins had become as it were nebulas, agglomerating subsidiaries like so many particles, dislocating them, relocating them, creating ramifications, distant arborescence, rootlets, muddling levels of participation, assets, and boards of directors, constructing a maze so intricate that it was no longer possible to know who was who and who did what. In such circumstances as these, digging down to foundations called for a degree of competence in economic archeology that far surpassed the Investigator's skills as well as his curiosity. He wondered why questions like those were even occurring to him. Quite definitely, he wasn't in his normal state. His fever was probably rising. The immense old man in the photograph was still looking down at him, but now it seemed to the Investigator that the man's smile had changed, had passed from benevolent to ironic.

All at once his eyelids became very heavy. He closed them for a fraction of a second, but when he reopened them, he saw that the office was plunged in darkness. The daylight that had been streaming in through the two big bay windows just a few instants previously had given way all at once to a night of deep, black, total darkness. And it had happened in the blink of an eye! Panic-stricken, he rose from the armchair and hurried over to the windows. Yes, night had fallen, all right. But if so, how long had his eyes been shut? Could he really have fallen asleep for several minutes, maybe even much longer? And in that case, where was the Manager? What time was it? He looked at his watch: 9:43 p.m.! He went to the door his host had disappeared through and knocked three times, then four, then five, harder and harder. No one responded. He put his ear to the wood. No sound, not even a tiny one, came from the other side of the door. He grabbed the doorknob and turned it, only to discover that the door was locked. He rattled the knob with increasing desperation.

"May I know what you're doing in this office at this hour?"

The Investigator froze. He could feel his blood turning to ice in his veins. Someone was standing a few yards behind him. Someone who had entered the room unheard.

"Put your hands in the air, very slowly, and turn around without making any sudden movements," the voice ordered, not cordially at all.

XXI

T HE INVESTIGATOR PIVOTED AROUND while raising his arms very high, hands open and well apart to show he wasn't holding a weapon.

"That's it, like that, very good," continued the voice, which the Investigator seemed to recognize. "Now, no more moving."

The man shined a flashlight on him. Its beam swept the Investigator from head to foot. "I'm going to turn on the light," the man said. "But remember, you're not to move. I'm armed, and if you make the slightest movement, it will be your last mistake. Understood?"

The Investigator, whose eyes were by this point at last accustomed to the darkness, felt like a laboratory mouse placed under light projectors for observation. He blinked his eyes and then, at the end of an extended moment, was finally able to make out the man who was taking aim at him.

"What? It's you?" the Investigator said with relief, recognizing the Guide and beginning to lower his hands.

"*No moving!* Keep your hands high!" said the Guide in a curt, hard tone. "I won't hesitate to shoot."

The Investigator knew he couldn't be mistaken. The man was indeed the Guide, the one who'd escorted him to that very office some hours earlier. It couldn't be anyone else, unless he had an identical twin. Only his clothes were different: The elegant gray double-breasted suit was replaced by a black jumpsuit with a zippered front, cinched at the waist with a canvas belt. In addition, he was wearing a soft cap, also black, and high-topped military boots. His right hand held a remarkably large revolver.

"But look, please," the Investigator stammered, "we know each other! You're the——"

"Not one more word, or I'll be forced to utilize my weapon!" the man yelled, rapidly approaching him and steadily aiming the revolver. When he got within reach of the Investigator, he flattened him against the wall and obliged him to put both hands behind his back. After cuffing them together with a plastic strap, he pushed him roughly toward the exit, taking care along the way to stop beside one of the armchairs, pick up the hard hat, and replace it on the Investigator's head.

That had all taken place in fewer than thirty seconds, and the Investigator had been unable to react or say a word. The man's handgun didn't look like a toy, and besides, whether it was or not, the Investigator felt too weak to offer any sort of resistance. Before leaving the room, the armed man gazed at the big photograph of the old fellow, and then, appearing to speak more to the portrait than to the Investigator, he said very loudly, *"The police have been informed and will be here soon! You will have to answer for what you've done!"*

At that, he shoved the Investigator into the hall and rushed out after him, quickly closing the door behind them.

"Good God . . . !" The man took several deep breaths, laughed a little nervously, looked at the Investigator, and used a knife to cut off his handcuffs. "I beg your pardon," he said, "but I had to play the game. That place must be loaded with microphones—and cameras, too, no doubt!"

The Investigator no longer had any idea what was going on. "I was sure you were going to give me away," the other said.

"Then you *are* the one who . . . you're the Guide?"

Suddenly the man appeared to be extremely annoyed. "Certainly not. After a certain hour, I become the Watchman . . . You see, my salary is so abysmally low . . . I hacked into the computer system and worked out a way to give myself both positions, but if anyone in the Central Directorate finds out, I'm sunk. . . . You won't say anything, will you? As I think you can tell, my situation is such that I'll stop at nothing. A desperate man has very little to lose."

As he said that, he shook his weapon in front of the Investigator's eyes, and he, with a wordless look, indicated that he'd keep the secret.

"I know of no other solution to my plight. It's humiliating, but what can you do? When you don't have what it takes to play a leading role, you have to take several small walk-on parts in order to survive. No, if you don't mind, please keep your hard hat on!"

The Investigator readjusted his headgear, not even trying anymore to understand why one person insisted that he wear it and another required him to take it off at once.

"But to hell with that, what about you? Why are you still in this office at this hour?"

Without going into details, the Investigator felt obliged to summarize what the Manager had said, but he kept quiet about the Manager's attempt to hurdle his desk and the pathetic display that had followed, with the Manager on his knees, weeping at the Investigator's feet. Then he described the Manager's abrupt departure, attributed by the Investigator to courtesy: The Manager, he explained, must have gone off to see about the Investigator's meal, which had been ordered but never received.

"Come on, what are you talking about? For the past fourteen months, the Enterprise's restaurant has been closed for renovations! As the Manager knows very well. It's caused a lot of discontent among the personnel—there's even the threat of a strike! How could he have made you such a promise? Are you certain you understood him correctly?"

The Investigator was no longer sure of anything. Not even his name. He shrugged his shoulders with an air of resignation.

"In any case," the other went on, "the Manager left the Enterprise quite a while ago. I personally saw him exit the tower in the late afternoon. Now, come on, you can't stay here. If someone finds you, that will necessarily mean trouble for me."

The Watchman, formerly the Guide, put his weapon back in its holster, gave the Investigator's shoulder a light tap, and signaled to him to follow. They went down the same winding stairway they'd gone up together several hours earlier. The first time, the Investigator had felt a pleasant giddiness as he climbed the stairs; on the way down, he was seized by an overwhelming feeling of nausea, which made the steel-and-aluminum structures of the tower look as soft as marshmallows. Sharp angles bent into curves, straight lines turned into moving coils, the stairs themselves became shaky, rubbery, incomparably treacherous, like a supple, mobile carpet of moss. The farther down he went, the more the world came apart, a little as though someone were dismantling a stage set that was no longer needed, and he understood that if he didn't quicken his pace, he'd no doubt risk being absorbed by that shifting, yielding, unstable mass, as surely as dirty water disappears into a gutter.

XXII

A FORCEFUL SLAP BROUGHT HIM BACK to consciousness.
"Pardon me, but I wasn't sure what to do. You literally collapsed against me at the bottom of the stairs. I
had to hold you up and drag you out, and as soon as we got
through the door, you dropped like a ripe fruit! Do you feel
any better?"

The Watchman was standing over the Investigator, who
lay curled up on the ground. There was no sympathy in the
Watchman's worried face, and nothing friendly in his question. The Investigator made a vague hand gesture to show
him there was no cause for alarm.

"You're not carrying some virus, by any chance, are you?"
asked the Watchman. "Because what the Enterprise really
doesn't need at this moment is an epidemic!"

"Nothing to fear," the Investigator murmured weakly.
"It's just that . . . I haven't eaten anything since yesterday
morning. . . ."

The Watchman seemed surprised: "Since yesterday
morning, you say?" He thought for a moment. "That's only
two days. You mustn't have a very solid constitution if a little
two-day fast can put you in this state. Either that, or you don't

have enough willpower. Six months ago, the Deputy Head of the Export Department went on a hunger strike. He said no one had the right to put him in a pre-retirement program. Guess how many days he held out?"

The Investigator shook his head to indicate that he had no idea.

"No, no, say a number!"

"Fifteen days . . . ?"

"Forty-two! He held out for forty-two days. Do you realize how long that is? Forty-two days! Management didn't want to give in. And they were right! *They were right not to give in!*"

He'd screamed the last sentence, looking all around as he did so. Then he fell silent, calmed down, and turned his eyes again to the Investigator, who was still on the ground. He began to feel the beneficial effects of fresh air.

"How did it end?"

"I beg your pardon?"

"The hunger strike you were talking about."

"Ah, right," said the Watchman, as if setting foot on a shore abandoned long ago. "The DHED died. Simply died. The organism has its limits. Forty-two days is a lot of days. Too many days. Some people never know when to stop. Result: no pre-retirement, plus no retirement at all. Nothing. So that's one less grumbler, and his position comes free and makes somebody happy."

"I never heard about that case," groaned the Investigator. "At least, I don't think so, it wasn't mentioned in the documents that—"

The Watchman violently interrupted him. "And why should you be informed that the Deputy Head of the Export

Department died while on a hunger strike? Why? Aren't you here to investigate the suicides? And only the suicides?"

"So I am," the Investigator said thoughtfully. "But perhaps, if you consider it, the course of action taken by the hunger striker might seem like a form of suicide. . . ."

The Watchman planted his legs a little wider apart, pushed his cap back on his head, folded his arms, and was quiet for several seconds. He appeared to be pondering something. Above him, the sky was as black as his uniform, so black that only his wide-open, furious eyes emerged from the darkness, or that was how it seemed to the Investigator. In the end, the Watchman unfolded his arms and, with a threatening look, pointed his right index finger down at the Investigator. "Tell me something," he said. "According to what you just said, you haven't eaten for two days. Doesn't that mean—if I follow your reasoning—doesn't that mean you're trying to commit suicide?"

The ground was covered by a not very thick layer of delicate, perfectly pure snow. The Investigator had just noticed it. Blackness covered the sky, and this white carpet was on the ground, and he was sitting on it. Wind buffeted his long white coat, which he was still wearing, carefully buttoned up, and which appeared to be keeping him pleasantly warm. The hard hat protected his balding head. He was freezing, certainly, and yet he wasn't cold, not cold at all. He even had the impression that he was languishing in palpable, unctuous heat. He could have fallen asleep there, in front of the entrance, yes, he could have slept there for hours and escaped from his situation, which made no sense.

The Watchman waited, his left fist against his hip, his right hand on the butt of his revolver.

"I'm hungry," the Investigator finally said. "I would eat anything, whatever I could get. I won't make a fuss, I swear to you. . . ."

The Watchman immediately relaxed, blew his breath out hard, took his hand off his weapon, and wiped his forehead. "Good God, you scared me! That was close! Yes, you just saved your life! I was on the point of deciding that you were a mole!"

"A mole?"

"Yes, I thought you'd been turned, if you prefer. It's a classic expression in espionage."

"But I'm not a spy, I'm the In—"

"I know perfectly well who you are, but you're missing the point. Consider: Someone is sent to investigate a wave of suicides, but he himself turns out to have dangerous, potentially suicidal tendencies; therefore, everything's distorted, the system sabotages itself, the whole shebang explodes, it's the end of all things! Now do you grasp my meaning?"

"Not very well . . ." the Investigator murmured. He could no longer feel his hands, which were thrust into the snow.

"It doesn't matter. But get up, for heaven's sake! You have to leave right away. You'll come back tomorrow."

The Watchman grabbed him, raised him to his feet, propped him against a wall, and then started rummaging in his own pockets. Eventually, he found what he was looking for and handed it to the Investigator. "Take that, it's all I've got."

The Investigator took hold of a largish stonelike object, brown and wrinkled, about four inches long, more or less round, and curved in the middle. He raised his eyes to the Watchman, not daring to formulate his question, but the latter anticipated him: "Top-quality. It may be a little dry. It's probably been forgotten in my uniform for the past three months, but I offer it with all my heart."

And as the Investigator hesitated before the thing he was holding in his hand, the Watchman became frosty again and asked in a suspicious tone, "On top of everything else, do you mean to tell me you don't eat pork?"

XXIII

T REMBLING WITH FEAR BUT FINALLY outside on the sidewalk, the Investigator turned around for a last glimpse
of the Guard. The latter didn't notice, however, as he'd
already gone back to his newspaper and sandwich. When
the Investigator looked at him, the Guard was the picture
of calm, tranquilly chewing and reading the sports page.

Earlier, inside the Enterprise, the Watchman had barely
spoken to the Investigator again after giving him the sausage. The snow covering the red, green, blue, and yellow
lines on the ground made them impossible to see, and the
Watchman had limited himself to indicating the way out by
mechanical gestures. When they were nearing the Guardhouse, the Watchman had stopped the Investigator and
ordered him to remove his white coat, hard hat, and badge.

"They'll be returned to you tomorrow," the Watchman
said. "Equipment belonging to the Enterprise cannot leave
the Enterprise."

The Investigator thrust his hands into his pockets, found
the key ring with the old man's photograph, and started to
return it to the Watchman. "No, keep it," he said. "It'll bring
you luck!"

Reluctantly, the Investigator handed over the heavy coat

and the too-small cap. It was a little as if he'd suddenly found himself naked, naked and frozen. His raincoat and suit were much too light and still too damp to protect him from the intensifying cold. "Yesterday," he said, "the Guard, I think, asked me if I had an Exceptional Authorization. Would it be possible for me to obtain one? I believe it could come in handy. . . ."

The Investigator went into a slight crouch, expecting a refusal, an outraged response, a sermon, perhaps some improbable—or hysterical—explanation, but the Watchman didn't say a word. From the top pocket of his jumpsuit he took a pen and from one of the side pockets a square piece of what looked like cardboard. He scribbled something on it and gave the document to the Investigator.

"There you are. I don't know what purpose an Exceptional Authorization may serve in your case, but you're welcome to it. And now I must ask you to excuse me. I have work to do."

He turned on his heel, walked away with long strides, and disappeared into the darkness and the swirling snow. The Investigator looked at what the Watchman had given him. It was a promotional coaster for a brand of beer. On the back of the stained, chipped square, the Watchman had written, "Exceptional Authorization granted to the holder of this card."

The Investigator was on the verge of calling him back, but he didn't have the strength. After all, the beer coaster fit in with all the rest. What else did he expect? He walked resolutely over to the Guardhouse, in which he could see some light, and in that light, a man's bent head.

The Investigator had to traverse some distance in order to get to the man, even though, in a straight line, he couldn't have been more than twenty yards away. But the caltrop barriers, the rolls of barbed wire, the chicanes, and the chevaux-de-frise, all of which were now back in place, were designed to create a labyrinthine passage that prevented precipitous exits as well as intrusions. Seeing that the Guard had noticed him and was observing his progress, the Investigator opted to solicit his favor with a little wave and a smile, but the movement caused the right side of his raincoat, the one with the torn and hanging pocket, to catch on the iron teeth of a piece of barbed wire, which summarily ripped a foot-long gash in the fabric. Inanimate matter is admirable; it knows no feelings, and therefore its existence is unencumbered by any weakness. You place it somewhere, and it performs its office. Only the elements, over the course of millennia, interfere with it, but it knows nothing of that. In spite of the accident, the Investigator kept a smile on his face. He didn't want the Guard to scrutinize him too closely, because it wouldn't have taken him long to notice that the Investigator looked like a tramp.

"Good evening!"

The Investigator needed to summon up all his remaining energy in order to pronounce those simple words in a natural tone of voice. The Guard was in the act of spreading the contents of a can of pâté on a demi-baguette. He was a nearly bald man with a roundish face. The newspaper in front of him, opened to the page with the sports scores, was strewn with bread crumbs. A half-empty bottle of wine stood next to an ashtray, in which a lit cigarette was smoking. Above the Guard's head and a little to his left, monitor screens displayed fixed images of different interior and exterior parts of the Enterprise. No human being appeared on any screen.

Those fragmentary images of the place gave a disturbing impression of unreality, as if surveillance cameras had been installed to watch over abandoned or never-used cinematic sets.

The Guard had raised his eyes and pressed the switch on his microphone. "Good evening!" he said. "Not too warm, is it?"

The Investigator was disconcerted by the Guard's cordial voice and relaxed air. He looked at the Investigator, smiling and continuing to slather his bread with the pâté, whose delicious fragrance filtered through the tiny perforations in the glass panel that separated them.

"I have an Exceptional Authorization!" the Investigator proclaimed, pressing the coaster against the glass.

The Guard glanced automatically at the piece of cardboard and then shifted his gaze to the Investigator. "I'm not sure what your Authorization authorizes you to do, but you look so proud to have it that I'm happy for your sake."

He took a large swig of wine, followed it with a last drag on his cigarette, crushed it out, and started eating his sandwich. The Investigator watched him with such longing that the other noticed it. "You look like you're in pitiful shape. Let me guess: This wasn't your lucky day, right?"

The Investigator nodded. The man's spontaneous kindness deeply moved him and almost made him forget his hunger. He felt his eyes getting misty.

"Go on, hurry back to your room, where it's nice and warm. Loitering around in this weather is only going to bring you grief. You've been exploited enough as it is, don't you think?"

The Guard took another bite of his sandwich. Although

the Investigator had no clear idea of what, or whom, the man was talking about, he took pleasure in drawing out this fraternal moment.

"What Department are you in?" asked the Guard. "Janitorial Services? You're a modern-day slave! One more! I hope at least you're not giving your all, are you? You and I, and thousands of others, we don't count for them. We're nothing. We're barely numbers on personnel lists. Some would find the situation depressing, but I couldn't care less. Look at me: The rule states that it's forbidden to smoke, drink, or eat while on duty; I do all three at the same time. I trample on the rule. They want to make us do crappy work no one wants to do? Then let's do a crappy job! I'm a free man. Since I've taken an immediate liking to you, I'm going to give you an example of what I mean: I'm a Guard, so therefore I'm supposed to protect the Enterprise from any and all unauthorized entry, right?"

The Investigator nodded. He'd lost control over the movements of his body, which was shaking with cold. On his head, a heavy accumulation of snow provided him with a curious hat. The Guard kept on talking while continuing to devour his sandwich. "I assure you that hundreds of individuals could come here with the intent of stealing everything not nailed down and I wouldn't lift my little finger to stop them, I'd let them through without pressing the least of the emergency buttons you see here in front of me. I daresay I'd open the gates even wider for them, and I'd applaud as they filled their trucks with whatever they could steal!"

The Guard took another big gulp of wine, straight from the bottle. "I don't mean to offend you," he went on, "but look at yourself. Do you see what a state they've reduced you to?

And all so they can keep raking in more profits! If I might give you a word of advice: A man in your position could cause some real damage. Instead of cleaning up their offices, you could sabotage all the computers. Oh, of course I don't mean by smashing them with a hammer, but by more discreet methods: a little water spilled on a keyboard, a cup of coffee in the ventilation grill of a hard-disk-drive cover, a tube of glue in a printer, the contents of your vacuum cleaner in the air-conditioning ducts, and maybe even a good old short-circuit now and then—the classics always work, that's why they're classics—and the whole thing collapses! The Enterprise is a colossus with feet of clay. Our world is a colossus with feet of clay. The problem is that few people like you— I mean little people, the exploited, the hungry, the weak, the contemporary slaves—few such people realize the truth. The time is past for taking to the streets and chopping off the heads of kings. There haven't been any kings for a long time. Today's monarchs don't have heads, or faces, either. They're complex financial mechanisms, algorithms, projections, speculations on risks and losses, fifth-degree equations. Their thrones aren't material thrones, they're screens, fiber optics, printed circuit boards, and their nobility is the encrypted information that circulates through them at speeds faster than light. Their castles have become databases. If you break one of the Enterprise's computers, one among thousands, you cut off one of the monarch's fingers. Do you understand?"

The Guard took another large mouthful of wine, gargling the liquid before swallowing it. The Investigator had listened to him with mouth agape, looking like a perfect idiot. The snow gave his thin shoulders a more marked, rectangular outline, thanks to which he became a sort of noncommissioned officer of the night, a stupefied sergeant in a routed army who'd been thrown into a conflict and could no longer recall the reason for the fighting. "Don't you think you ought to be more careful about what you say?" he ventured to ask.

"Careful? Why? For whose sake? I have no master. I know no authority. People like me still exist. Why do you think I do this job that everyone else refuses? Because I don't want to play the game. Look at me, behind this glass. I'm a total symbol! But wait, you're not a policeman, are you? Eh?"

"Of course not," said the Investigator.

"And the person who claims to be the Investigator—you're not him, either, right? My colleague warned me about this guy. He tried to force his way in here last night, around ten o'clock. His pretext was an Investigation into the suicides. An Investigation into the suicides at ten o'clock at night—do they think we're *that* stupid? I'm convinced this individual is actually a Downsizer. Another one. We get one a month. And every time, there are layoffs right and left. Those people have no morals—you realize that, don't you? If we'd let them, they'd come here even at night so they could get an early start on their repulsive tasks! Of course you're not the Investigator. With your miserable face, those three little hairs on your head, and your rags, you're like me, you're not him!"

"Of course not . . ." replied the Investigator, trembling—not solely from the cold—and clutching, in his raincoat's one remaining pocket, the old sausage that had been the Watchman's gift to him.

"I swear to you that if that individual comes back tonight," the Guard began again, "I won't be as amiable as my colleague. I'll fry him!"

"You'll . . . *fry* him?"

"Without batting an eye! You see that lever?" said the Guard, pointing to a kind of rubber-coated handle set into the wall. "If I pull it down, I send a twenty-thousand-volt current into all the metal barriers you see around you. Even if he doesn't touch them, even if he stands still in the place where you're standing right now, for example, the amperage is so high that in two or three seconds the repugnant creature will be reduced to a common heap of ashes!"

"A heap of ashes . . ." the Investigator groaned.

"Ashes to ashes, dust to dust!" the Guard concluded. A tiny morsel of pâté had fallen from his sandwich and now adorned his chin.

XXIV

RDINARILY, THE INVESTIGATOR DIDN'T dream much. His
nights were calm, and in the morning, he only rarely
remembered his dreams—except for the recurrent one
about the copy machine. He was in his office. He needed to
create a duplicate copy of an Investigation dossier. He went
to the room where the photocopier was located and started
to reproduce the documents in the dossier, but the toner
cartridge was almost out of ink, and the machine quickly
put itself into pause mode. Since he didn't know how to
change the cartridge—his function was to conduct successful Investigations, not to maintain photocopy machines—he
stood there helplessly, with no idea what to do. Most fortunately, that distressing dream had never become reality. But
this—that is to say, everything that had happened to him
since he'd set foot in this town—was quite obviously a nightmare. What else could it be? Nothing else. Yes, a nightmare.
A long nightmare, certainly diabolical in its complex, subtle,
convoluted realism, but a nightmare nonetheless!

The problem was that the Investigator couldn't perceive
any way out. He had no blessed idea about how to escape
from the world he was in, even though it was necessarily,
indubitably false, totally oneiric, utterly unlike life. Real life

couldn't be this bewildering, he thought, it couldn't throw you together with characters as disturbing as the ones who'd been having their fun with him since the previous evening, taking pleasure in starving him, battering him, disorienting him, stringing him along, crushing him, frightening him. But what if . . . ? What if . . . ? Maybe life—which up until that moment he'd experienced as a monotonous and pleasantly boring sequence of repetitions, without surprises— maybe life, considered from a certain perspective and in certain circumstances, entailed unforeseen, harrowing, or even tragic accidents.

The street was empty, as it had been the previous evening. The vehicles and the throngs of pedestrians had all disappeared, which hardly surprised him, and that was what he found truly amazing: He wasn't surprised anymore. He told himself he was starting to adopt the illogical logic of his nightmare. This didn't assuage his hunger or lower his fever or mend his raincoat or relieve his immense fatigue, but he felt a little better all the same. He reasoned that if his thoughts were patterning themselves after things that had happened to him and would no doubt go on happening to him, then he'd probably be better able to bear them, just as a man who's climbing up to high altitudes eventually becomes accustomed to the lack of oxygen.

Despite his great exhaustion and his weakened state, he crossed the street in a few seconds. The ease with which he did this made him snigger, remembering the difficulty he'd had that very morning getting to the entrance of the Enterprise. He headed for the Hotel, whose sign was trying to light up. The effort lasted a few seconds before the sign crackled wretchedly and then went out, only to begin a new attempt, doomed to failure like the others. The street was covered with snow, and the only tracks in it were his. This seemed to him proof that what he'd felt before was true: The snow was a dream; he was dreaming the street. It couldn't possibly be unmarked by vehicle tracks and untrodden by pedestrian traffic, for the City was densely populated, as he'd verified for himself that morning, when hundreds of cars and thousands of people had clogged the street. He was, therefore, dreaming.

But there were holes in his reasoning, and he was seized by doubt. He saw that he was hedging his bets between dream and reality, choosing one or the other, whichever suited him, to explain events. His lovely nightmare theory fell apart. There was, alas, only one reality, and he was stuck in it up to the neck, like a wooden stick in a barrel of molasses. A few minutes earlier, his morale had begun to recover, but now it collapsed, a fragile house of cards. His headache was very bad again.

He was exhausted when he pushed open the door of the Hotel. The Giantess was behind the reception counter. Upon seeing him, she said, "You *were* in room 14, correct?"

The Investigator couldn't utter so much as a word. He contented himself with a nod of his head, wondering what might be the significance of that past-tense verb. What register had he been expunged from? What list had he been crossed off of? And why? As before, the Giantess was wearing her pink terry-cloth bathrobe, which totally enveloped her massive body. The Investigator felt tiny in her presence. Despite his cold and the few yards that still separated him from the desk, he was able to detect the big woman's sweet, sweaty scent.

"We've been obliged to change your room. The Management apologizes sincerely for any inconvenience. Your new room is number 93. Second floor. Your bag's already inside." The Giantess placed a very small key on the counter in front of the Investigator. He was about to take the key, but she held it down with her index finger. "One more thing," she said, using her free hand to place a document on the counter. "I need you to sign this bill for the property destruction you caused this morning."

"Property destruction . . . ?"

"An official report transmitted to me specifies damages in the ladies' restroom on this floor. I'm simply passing the bill on to you. I make no judgment in regard to your presence in a ladies' room. . . ."

The Giantess had spoken the last sentence in a lighter tone, a tone full of insinuation. The Investigator nearly launched into explanations, but then he changed his mind. What good would explaining do? He took hold of the bill and the pen the Giantess had placed on the counter and prepared to sign. But when he saw the total amount written on the bill, he recoiled. "This can't be possible!" he exclaimed. "All these charges for a torn towel? I refuse to sign such a document!"

He slammed the pen down on the counter, but this had no effect on the Giantess, who continued to watch him impassively. The Investigator found her steady gaze unsettling. He took up the bill again and examined it in greater detail. It contained fifteen items: *replacement of destroyed towel, replacement of destroyed towel dispenser, replacement of destroyed screws, replastering of damaged wall, repainting of damaged wall, meals for three workers (plasterer, painter, carpenter), transportation expenses for said three workers, cleanup of worksite, disinfection of toilets, initial report fee, certified statement fee, general expenses tax, secondary expenses tax, taxes tax, taxes tax tax.*

"That's simply robbery! First your fake Policeman makes me waste my entire morning, and now you're telling me I—"

"What fake Policeman?" the Giantess asked, interrupting him.

Summoning all his remaining strength, the Investigator fought back the cloying nausea that rose to his lips, swallowed hard, and pressed his hands against his temples to lessen the pain that was beating inside his skull with the persistence of a percussionist. "I'm sure you know him better than I do. The man who lives in that broom closet there," the Investigator said, pointing to the small room where the Policeman had taken his statement.

The Giantess looked at the door of the storage room and then at the Investigator again. "I can't go on," he said. "I have to get some sleep. We'll see about all this tomorrow. Just give me back my ID and credit card. . . ."

"Where are they?"

Choking with panic, the Investigator said, "What do you mean? They're in that box there! You confiscated them from me last night and put them in that box! Remember?"

The Giantess froze, appeared to stop breathing, and kept staring fixedly at him. "I don't remember," she said. "I don't remember anything when my sleep is interrupted at 3:14 a.m. Moreover, 'confiscated' isn't the proper word. As you no doubt recall, the Rules—"

"Paragraph eighteen, line C . . ."

"Exactly. We've already had enough problems with clients who take a room without being able to pay for it."

"Give me back what belongs to me . . . please," the Investigator implored her, putting all his distress into his words. The Giantess seemed to be shaken by his plea. She hesitated and then slowly slid her right hand down the front of her nightgown between her breasts, felt around for a moment, and pulled out a golden key. She slipped it into the lock on the front of the little box, gave it three complete counterclockwise turns, opened the metal door, and looked inside.

"Well? What was it you wanted to get back?" she asked in a mocking tone. The Investigator didn't take his eyes off the box.

It was tragically empty.

XXV

T HE INVESTIGATOR ALMOST LOST HIS GRIP for good.
There was a long minute during which he felt that his
head and body were on the point of coming apart, of
splitting open like a wall shaken by an earthquake, or by the
shock wave of an extremely powerful bomb. He shut his eyes
to cancel the sight of the empty box, which contained absolutely nothing and so became, in a way, a perfect metaphor
for the situation he found himself in, or even for his entire
life. Then, with his eyes still closed, he heard himself speak.
Yes, words were issuing from his mouth, words like groans,
weak, hesitant, convalescent, barely audible words, as if
they'd taken roundabout routes on their way to the Giantess,
bypasses, detours, side paths, endless highways, losing at each
turning a little of their strength and much of their texture.

"How is this possible? You require me to entrust important documents to you, and then you lose them?"

The Giantess's voice reached him where he stood in his
darkness. "Well, that's what you say, but I repeat, I don't
remember anything. I was asleep when you arrived."

"But how about me? Do you remember me?"

"Very vaguely, to tell you the truth. And that doesn't
prove anything. I was told to wait for room 14 to come in this

evening. You were the only Guest who hadn't returned yet. So, when you came in a little while ago, I concluded that you were number 14. I didn't make that deduction based on your appearance—you have no distinguishing features."

The Investigator opened his eyes. "Are you the only person who has a key to that box?"

"My daytime Colleague has the other one."

"Could he have put my credit card and identification somewhere else?"

The Giantess hesitated. "It's unlikely."

"Unlikely but not impossible," replied the Investigator. He was at the very end of his strength, but he perceived a ray of hope.

"I repeat: unlikely."

"Could we verify that tomorrow? I really need to sleep. I'm so weak. I've eaten nothing. Nothing."

The Giantess frowned as if she suspected a dirty trick. "And how are you going to pay if you don't have any money?"

The Investigator's arms dropped to his sides. Couldn't he find some respite, however brief, in the impossible situation he was in? "I was sent here on a mission," he said, conscious that the statement made him sound like one of those lunatics who frequent the centers of megalopolises, proclaiming to all and sundry that they are the messengers of God or of some extraterrestrial race. "I have an Investigation to conduct," he went on, striving to adopt a natural tone. "An Investigation into the Enterprise, which is located just across from your establishment."

"Then you would be . . . the Investigator?" the Giantess asked in surprise.

"Absolutely."

The Giantess hesitated, walked around her counter, went up to him, grasped him gently by the shoulder, turned him around to examine him in detail, and then pushed him toward the big mirror that covered one of the walls in the entrance. "Look at yourself."

In the glass the Investigator saw a stooped old man with a two-day beard and hot, bloodshot eyes rolling incessantly from left to right and from right to left. His swollen forehead had turned an orangey yellow, and the area surrounding the wound caused by the falling telephone was now purple. The clothes he had on were rags, crumpled, soiled, and torn, particularly his raincoat, which must once have been a decent example of its kind. There was also a sizable slash in his trousers at the level of his right thigh. The flesh was visible, naked and white except for a long, zigzagging scratch stained with dried blood. His shoes were like big clumps of brownish lint. On one, the front half of the sole had come unglued, and the other was missing its shoelace.

"Who do you expect to believe that you look like the Investigator?"

"But I don't have to look like the Investigator, I *am* the Investigator!" he said, addressing himself as much as the Giantess. "I'm the Investigator . . ." he repeated softly, as if to bolster his own conviction, while big tears welled in his eyes, full, round tears that rolled down his face and slid toward the wrinkled skin of his neck. A child's tears. He remained like that in front of the mirror for a moment, incapable of moving, incapable of the smallest reaction. The Giantess went back to her post behind the counter.

"Sign the bill for me," she said, "and then you can go to your room. Since you've just informed me that you're not in a position to settle your Hotel bill and that you don't even have a piece of identification, I could turn you out into the street, but I'm not a cruel woman, and I'm sure we'll be able to come to some sort of an arrangement."

He turned slowly toward the Giantess, took the pen she held out to him, and signed the bill without even looking at it.

"You're forgetting your key!"

He was already on his way to the stairs. He went back, picked up the room key—in doing so, he had to graze the Giantess's large, damp fingers—and very slowly climbed up the stairs, holding tightly to the handrail.

Tomorrow, he'd make a call. Yes, he'd ring up his Head of Section. Things couldn't go on this way, and if his boss thought him stupid or incompetent, too bad. In any case, he wasn't going to let this job cost him his health, whether mental or physical, to say nothing of his skin. He'd explain everything. The Head of Section would understand, make things right with the Hotel, and stand security for the Investigator, and then everything would return to normal. He'd feel better in the morning, and the first thing he'd do, of course, would be to change hotels. He wouldn't stay another night in this one. He'd forget it. He'd dismiss it from his life.

The Investigator stood before the door of room 93. It was indeed located on the second floor, just as the Giantess had told him. He turned the key and pushed the door, which wouldn't open more than about eight inches, despite his repeated efforts. With difficulty, he slipped into the narrow space, flipped the light switch, and discovered the room: a single bed, a night table, an armoire, a chair, a closed window through which he could see closed shutters. There was a door that led, no doubt, to the bathroom. The furnishings were the same as those in room 14; the walls were the same greenish color, blistered by dampness; the light was the same, an exhausted, intermittent, circular neon tube; and there was the same photograph of the old man, so much like the one on the key ring. The only difference regarded the size of the room: Here, the floor space was exiguous, and almost all of it was occupied by the bed. It blocked both the armoire door and the door of the bathroom, access to which, therefore, was strictly impossible. As for the chair and the night table, instead of standing on the floor, they had been laid on their sides across the bed, next to his suitcase.

The Investigator closed the door behind him. "Hold on," he exhorted himself, clenching his fists. "Hold on . . . hold on. At least get through the night."

He climbed onto the bed and pushed the night table and the chair as far as possible toward the bottom of the mattress. Then he grabbed his suitcase, lifted it with difficulty because it was so heavy—or was it, rather, that he was exhausted?— managed to raise it overhead, and tried unsuccessfully, three times, to slide it onto the top of the armoire. When he realized that the space between the ceiling and the armoire was smaller than the suitcase, he gave up the effort.

He released the suitcase, which fell heavily to the bed and in doing so caused a small cylindrical object that had apparently been covered by a fold of the bedspread to bounce into the air, a bit like a little horned devil springing up out of a jack-in-the-box. The object was a small yellow-and-blue medicine bottle, the same as the one containing pain medication that the Policeman had given him that very morning. The Investigator picked up the little bottle, clutched it in one quivering hand, and felt a knot in his throat. So he wasn't a totally bad person after all, the so-called Policeman, because he'd thought about the Investigator, he'd been concerned about the state of his health, he'd taken the trouble to put the medicine on the Investigator's bed himself. It had to have been him; no one else would or could have done that. Only him.

The Investigator smiled weakly and then lay down on the bed, once again without taking the trouble to undress. He rolled onto his side, drew his knees up to his stomach, tucked his chin into one shoulder, and closed his eyes.

Immediately he plunged into a deep sleep, holding the medicine bottle and the dry sausage, one in each hand: an old sausage, desiccated and inedible, and a medicine bottle containing tablets he couldn't even take because he had no water and couldn't get into the bathroom. The two items, in short, were unequivocally of no use, but they nonetheless bore witness to a touching human possibility in a world that appeared to him more and more unfounded.

XXVI

Something was ringing. A timorous, quavering, tired sound. The telephone. Like the previous morning. A little light was coming in through the closed shutters. The telephone. The Investigator opened his eyes. How small the room was, and how narrow! He felt as though he'd slept in a box. The ringing continued, but he couldn't see any telephone. Where could it be, damn it? Nothing on the walls. Nothing on the armoire, or on the door of the armoire, or on the bathroom door. The ringing, though exceedingly weak, didn't give up. Under the bed? Could someone have been so irrational as to put a telephone under a bed? No, nothing down there. The ringing went on. He pressed one ear against the armoire door, which he wouldn't have been able to open in any case, but the ringing wasn't coming from inside the armoire. The ceiling? The ceiling was all that was left! Could the telephone be attached to the ceiling? The ringing, timid but regular, persisted. The Investigator was on all fours on the bed. He didn't want to look up; it was simply inadmissible that someone could have installed a telephone on the ceiling. The ringing didn't stop. He resigned himself to tilting his head slowly upward, and there was the telephone, mounted a little to the left of the circular neon light.

He bounded to his feet on the bed, stretched out his arms toward the telephone, tried to reach the receiver clipped to its cradle, missed it, dislodged it on his third try, and caught it as it yo-yoed at the end of its rubber cord.

"Hello?"

"Hello?" replied a muffled voice, terribly far away.

"Can you hear me?" the Investigator asked.

"Can you hear me?" the voice repeated.

"Who is this?"

"Who is this?" the distant voice answered.

"I'm the Investigator."

"I can't take it anymore!" the distant voice said. "I can't open it."

"Open what?"

"It's horrible, it's absolutely impossible to open!"

"Open what?" the Investigator hollered.

"Impossible . . . I've tried everything. And it's so hot! Help me . . ." the voice stammered, dying down.

"Are you still there?"

"I'll never be able to leave. . . . It's impossible."

"But leave what? Where? Who are you?"

"Like a rat . . ." said the voice, and then it fell silent.

The Investigator looked at the receiver. No more words were audible, but the telephone hadn't been hung up; he could still hear breathing. However, there was no longer anything human about that breathing. It sounded like wind blowing over a flat, desolate landscape. Who was the caller? Was he the same man who'd called him the previous morning? How could he find out? And what could he do? Not a thing, no doubt about that. Someone must be watching his movements. This was all a joke, only a joke.

After a few seconds, he stood on tiptoe, reached up to the base of the telephone, which was screwed to the ceiling, and put the receiver back on the hook; and at that moment, only at that moment, did he realize that he was completely naked.

An idiotic reflex made him cover his groin with both hands. But who could see him? The room had only one window, and the closed shutters protected him from any prying eyes. Besides, even though he didn't wish to verify his conviction, he was positive that he'd find the same concrete-block wall behind the shutters in this room as he had in room 14.

Why was he naked? He wasn't in the habit of sleeping in the nude. The Investigator felt so ashamed that he hid himself, head and body, under the bedcovers. All the same, he couldn't stay there indefinitely. He rolled on the bed, wrapping the sheet around him, got to his feet on the mattress, and started looking for his clothes. He found the old sausage and the medicine bottle without difficulty, but there was no trace of his undershirt, his undershorts, his shoes, his shirt, his trousers, his suit jacket, or his raincoat. Vanished, evaporated, gone without trace. And yet they had to be there somewhere.

The Investigator tried to remember where he might have put his clothes, but since he was utterly unable to recall getting undressed, it was all the more difficult for him to figure out what he'd done with them. His interior dialogue came to an end with a violent sneeze, then another, then a third. His stopped-up, running nose obliged him to breathe through his mouth, at an elevated rate, so that he looked like a goldfish imprisoned in a bowl. A boiling-hot shower, or even an ice-cold one, wouldn't do him any harm, he thought. It would give him a boost, stimulate his mind, invigorate his body. All he had to do was get into the bathroom!

Wrapped in his sheet, which gave him the air of a short, round-bellied Roman senator, the Investigator thought awhile before coming up with a plan he put into action without delay. The plan called for him to lift up the bed as high as possible—as high as his puny muscles would permit—to wedge the night table under it, and then, if he still had the strength, to raise the bed even higher, jamming the chair between the night table and the bed frame. In the end, the bed was standing nearly vertically on one side, and the bathroom door was free.

He could open it.

XXVII

To his great astonishment, he found the bathroom a model of refined luxury. He'd never have suspected that such a grandiose space, its walls decorated with pale-green mosaics topped by a fretwork frieze of studs gilded with fine gold, could exist within the precincts of the Hope Hotel; the bathroom was probably the sole remaining vestige of a time when the establishment really did provide first-class lodging. And to think, this sumptuous bathroom came with the room he'd been put in, which was, as he could certify, incontestably the narrowest, nastiest, wretchedest room in the Hotel—it was a mystery that passed his understanding!

A pearly light caressed the heavy gold fixtures of the two sinks, the bidet, the large bathtub—which had been hollowed out of a block of porphyry—and the shower, a spacious enclosure completely covered with bluish glass-paste tiles. From multiple loudspeakers—none of which he was able to locate, but which seemed to have been built into the walls—came music that mingled the cries of exotic birds, a gently stroked tambourine, soft brasses mimicking the sound of small coins falling on a stone floor, and flutes simultaneously shrill and mellow. In the center of the room, a small fountain threw up a stream of water, whose blithe gurgling and steamy vapor sent the Investigator into a reverie of distant seaports, of black and naked female slaves, of palm fronds wielded to cool his brow, of big ships anchored in the harbor, of their ebony macassar-wood decks laden with sacks of spices, pearls, amber, and bitumen. He'd been compelled to read a little poetry for school assignments in his youth, but he'd never understood any of it. And what he'd found especially hard to understand was that men could waste their time writing poems, which served no useful purpose, none at all; cold, precise investigative reports written to give an account of proven facts, to narrow a search for truth, and to draw valid conclusions struck him as a more intelligent—indeed, as the only valid—way of using language and serving humanity. How ill and unnerved must he be, that the mere sight of an opulent bathroom could set him daydreaming about languorous Negresses and palm wine, Oriental pastries and belly dances?

A set of crystal shelves held bottles of multicolored bath salts and liquid soap. The Investigator opened a few and tried to inhale their scent, but his cold was so severe that he could smell nothing at all. He settled for reading the labels and decided on Mauve Lilac.

He let the sheet fall. Once again totally naked, but not feeling the slightest embarrassment on that account, the Investigator poured the entire contents of the soap bottle into his hands and rubbed the liquid into his remaining hair and over his face and body. Then he turned on the two faucets in the shower, and at once a generous stream of water rained down, giving off a vapor that the opalescence of the glass-paste tiles turned blue.

He thrust his right foot into the shower, shouted in sudden pain, and quickly drew back: The water was boiling!

Not hot, but boiling! He closed the hot water faucet a little, opened the cold water faucet almost all the way, waited, and then ventured again to stick his foot into the cascade. It was even worse! He felt as though molten lead were being poured onto his flesh. He abandoned the shower for the bathtub, turned on the tap, waited: Clouds of steam rose at once from the porphyry block, and he didn't dare put his foot in. He made do with holding one hand close to the water and determined that it, too, was flowing out at an atrociously high temperature. His only remaining choices were the sinks and the bidet. He hurried over to them and turned on the faucets, mixing a little hot water with a great deal of cold. Wasted effort: The water that came out of those faucets could have cooked an egg in thirty seconds. It was then that he examined the pipes and came to the astounding conclusion that there was no cold-water pipe leading to any tap in the bathroom.

Even in the basin of the little fountain, the water, whose fine vapor he'd taken for the product of some sort of sophisticated atomizing system, was at the boiling point, as indicated by the three Japanese carp floating belly-up in it, their flesh white, cooked, and already disintegrating.

The beauty of the bathroom served no useful purpose. It was a Paradise warmed by the flames of Hell. Washing oneself in it was impossible, just as it was impossible to dry oneself, since there was no towel and no bathrobe. His body entirely coated with sticky, redolent Mauve Lilac, the Investigator felt his recent and very modest upsurge in optimism plunging down again. At the moment when he stooped to gather up his bedsheet, a door opened behind him, and a big, heavily mustachioed man in his seventies entered, passed close to him, sat on the toilet, unfolded a newspaper, and began to read.

The Investigator dared not move. Where had this old man come from? He was absolutely naked, just like him; he'd practically grazed him without even noticing; and he resembled, feature for feature, the old fellow on the Enterprise key rings, the one whose immense photographic portrait adorned the Manager's office, the one whose image was reproduced in the pictures that hung in the Hotel rooms. Was this really the same person? It was difficult to say; people, whether naked or clothed, make such different impressions. And what immodesty! Whoever he was, his behavior was unbelievable. To come in like that and sit down on the toilet!

The Investigator was on the verge of calling out when it occurred to him that perhaps it was he himself who was not in his proper place. Suppose this bathroom wasn't his? After all, hadn't he had to expend a considerable amount of effort and ingenuity to unblock a door that had no doubt been barricaded on purpose? But, yes, of course, that was it—he wasn't where he ought to be. His only thought was to get out, to get out at once, before the septuagenarian noticed his presence and caused a scandal.

The old man was thoroughly absorbed in his newspaper. A benevolent smile brightened his wrinkled face. The Investigator straightened up, very slowly. Then, equally slowly, he slid his feet inch by inch toward the door of his room, but when he reached it, he couldn't open it. He didn't try too hard, for fear of alerting the old man, who kept on reading and paid no attention to him. The Investigator resolved that his salvation lay in the only other exit, the door through which the old man had come in. It was directly opposite the spot he'd just laboriously reached, at the cost of great pain in his toes, particularly those on his scalded right foot, which had turned scarlet. But he had no other choice. He therefore set out again, smeared head to foot with Mauve Lilac, and, after a ploddingly slow slide across the marble floor, he reached the other door, opened it in silence, and disappeared.

XXVIII

T HE ROOM HE CROSSED, almost running, was very different from his. Like the bathroom he'd just left, it was vast, luxurious, and comfortable, with a look of extreme refinement. He had just enough time to notice a cabin trunk that was standing open, revealing four or five suits, apparently all of them tailored from the same warm, supple fabric, a green-and-beige tweed. He also spotted a big cigar, about to burn itself out in an ashtray, weaving slate-gray coils into the room's conditioned air.

The Investigator found himself in the corridor, enveloped in his sheet. Or, rather, as he quickly determined, in *a* corridor. A corridor that he didn't recognize, but which was fortunately deserted. Where was his room? To the right? To the left? Logically, it had to be to the left, but since nothing in the Hotel obeyed established rules, it was extremely probable that his room was to the right. He turned that way, trying his luck, but as he advanced, dragging his poached right foot, the numbers he read on the doors of the rooms—765, 3, 67B, 5674, 1.6, A45718, BTH2Z—gave him no clue about the location of his own. He went back, passed again in front of the old man's room—ooooo@ooooo—and discovered that number 93, his room, was right next door to it. So he'd sent himself on a wild-goose chase with his convoluted reasoning! He went in.

The damages to the room were catastrophic. The wooden chair had eventually broken under the pressure of the bed, which had pivoted on its side and toppled over, striking the telephone on its way down and ripping it from the ceiling, along with the neon tube, before smashing the night table and staving in the door of the armoire. Destabilized by the blow, the armoire had fallen onto its side, blocking the door that led to the old man's bathroom.

Exhausted, the Investigator slid down to the floor and curled himself up with his head resting on his knees. Shaken by nervous spasms, in despair at what he considered the hopelessness of his situation, he felt like crying, but his body wouldn't let him, as if it, too, had joined his tormentors. He would have liked to be no more. Yes, to disappear. How strange human desires are sometimes. Even though men fear death, they often consider it a solution to their problems, without even realizing that it solves nothing. Absolutely nothing. It doesn't have to solve anything at all. That's not its role.

He felt something a little cool against his right thigh and opened his eyes: It was the medicine bottle left by the Policeman. He picked it up, gazed at it for a few seconds without managing to conceive the smallest thought in its regard, opened it, dumped all the tablets into his mouth, and started to chew them. Taken without water, they had a taste like aromatic herbs, pleasant and fresh. He reduced them to a slightly bitter pulp, which he then swallowed.

The room looked like a tiny battlefield. As such, it became an image, but of what combat? And if there had been a combat, who was the victor, and who was the vanquished?

The Investigator imagined the bill the Giantess wouldn't fail to present to him. It would, he was sure, amount to a good part of his savings. Maybe even the whole of them. Strangely enough, the prospect didn't bother him. He invested money without much knowing why, without even the desire to make use of it. At the end of every year, he had a meeting with the Financial Counselor, a man who would explain to him, with the aid of curves and diagrams, the most comfortable places for his money to nestle, places where it could nap in all tranquillity, like a pet, surrounded by all affection and necessary care, and where it would, beyond the shadow of a doubt and under the best possible conditions, reproduce itself. He didn't understand much of what he was being told, but in the end he would agree to the Counselor's proposals. Like most of his contemporaries, therefore, he was getting ready to die with money put aside. All at once, he realized the absurdity of that situation. If he had a little money, why keep it? For whom? Let it serve some useful purpose, like paying for damages! Why not?

As if to illustrate all those unaccustomed thoughts, grating on a brain accustomed to less effort, the Investigator sprang to his feet, seized the back of the demolished chair, and used it to complete the destruction of the premises, reducing the neon tube to glass powder, shattering the telephone's plastic shell, smashing the armoire, disemboweling mattress and eiderdown. He finished the job by taking hold of what remained of the night table, throwing it against the window—glass shards showered down on the devastated bed—and methodically laying waste whatever was intact in the room. Then he stopped, a little out of breath, but perfectly happy.

A violent energy, risen from unsuspected depths, electrified him. For the first time in his life, he'd performed a gratuitous act, and he wasn't at all sorry. On the contrary, when he imagined what the Policeman's face would look like when someone showed him the battlefield, the Investigator laughed a good deal. He'd decided that he was going to take back control of the situation, whatever it might be. He had an Investigation to conduct, and he would conduct it. He wasn't going to let a few fairly deranged individuals, an impossible hotel, a shameless old man, a hostile city, and an enterprise, even the Enterprise itself, get the best of him. Wrecking his room was an affirmation of his freedom. History, he thought, crushes only those who are willing to be crushed.

He cleaned himself as best he could, using his sheet to remove from his skin the hardened, cracked, whitish crust left there by the Mauve Lilac. He opened his suitcase to take out some clean clothes. The fact that it contained a drill, a set of bits for wood, another set for metal, and a third for concrete, along with five pairs of women's underpants, two brassieres, a Bible in Dutch, some apple-green sweatpants, a pair of rubber boots, a canary-yellow woolen dress, and three handkerchiefs that he recognized as his own, failed to diminish his newly regained vitality in the least. The Bellhop who'd cleared out his former room—as he had doubtless done with many others—had simply mixed up the personal belongings of several different Guests and then redistributed them at random to the various suitcases.

Without the slightest embarrassment, the Investigator slipped on a pair of the panties—pink synthetic fabric, with a delicate black lace trim—the jogging pants, the boots, and the yellow dress, which when sliced in half was miraculously transformed into a pleasantly warm sweater. After some little hesitation, he ultimately decided to leave the drill in the suitcase, telling himself that the tool would be more an encumbrance than anything else. On a hook fastened to the inside of the door, he found his raincoat, which someone had hung there. It had been cleaned and pressed, and it was protected by a thin plastic cover. An expert, faithful hand had mended the torn pocket and the big rip on the side. A piece of paper was pinned to the raincoat: *With the compliments of the Management.*

His heart was beating a hundred miles an hour. Throughout his body, he felt electric discharges contracting his muscles, including those of his face and eyelids, surprisingly and deliciously. It promised to be a fine day, he was certain of it. He was no longer simply a vapid, weak, drab character, profoundly distressed by a sequence of events he couldn't understand. He was no longer just the Investigator. He was becoming a hero. He'd emancipated himself, he'd rebelled, he'd seized the power he'd been denied. The mouse would kill the cat. Chemistry was working miracles in him.

He left the room, violently slamming the door; the doorknob remained in his hand. He bounced it on his palm for a few seconds, negligently, rather like a fruit he was about to bite, and threw it over his shoulder, whistling. Then he went down the uneven stairs, two by two, on his way to the breakfast room.

XXIX

Y OU'RE IN ROOM 93?" asked a Server wearing white tails
and black pants.

"Absolutely!" the Investigator heard himself reply,
in a revivified voice. With a gesture, the Server invited him
to follow.

The breakfast room was once again packed with people,
but the Investigator recognized that they weren't the same as
those who'd filled the room the previous day. This morning
there were a lot of families, with children of all ages, including infants, and also many very old persons. They were all
poorly dressed, in clothes that were often far from ordinary:
Many of the men wore enormous, shabby robes that trailed
on the ground, big, threadbare sheepskin jackets, or faded,
sleeveless anoraks; the majority of the women had on black,
cone-shaped coats, buttoned down the front from throat to
feet. Headgear included knotted scarves, handmade ski caps,
fur hats, felt toques, seedy-looking berets, decrepit bowlers.

The people were all tightly clutching bundles, or distended, pathetic imitation-leather gym bags, or cardboard
boxes tied up with string, or enormous plastic sacks, many
of them held together with brown adhesive tape, or ancient
pasteboard suitcases that looked to be at the bursting point.

Most of the individuals shared physical traits: angular faces, small stature, pronounced noses, olive or frankly gingerbread complexions, dark curly hair, mauve-circled eyes that their evident state of exhaustion made seem even larger.

It was a welter of bodies.

The Investigator couldn't get over it. There were even more people than there had been the previous day. It seemed that the floor must crack under their weight. And what struck him with even greater force was the heavy silence that reigned in the spacious room. Those women, those men, those children, those old people—it was as if fatigue had sealed their lips and suppressed their desire to communicate.

They looked like peasants or workers or day laborers or farmhands from another century, beasts of burden whose bodies, unceasingly subjected to undernourishment and the law of work, were compelled to make do with their meager bones and the bit of flesh that covered them. Everything about the breakfast throng betrayed poverty, indigence, as well as the dread which that condition—no doubt undergone for decades or even centuries—had succeeded in depositing at the deepest level of their every movement, of every look in their eyes, like a genetic trait it's no use struggling against. The same mark, the mark of the downtrodden, was imprinted on each of those creatures. But nothing allowed the observer to identify their origins unequivocally or to name the exact country they came from.

Most of them were gathered in dense clusters around tables intended to seat four. For lack of room, skinny children sat on the laps of adults scarcely bigger than they were. They were nibbling on rusks the Investigator recognized, rusks identical to the appalling things he'd been obliged to consume the previous morning, and next to them stood little cups of black coffee, scantily filled with a muddy brew the mere memory of which nauseated him. So all those people, every one of them inhumanly thin whatever their age or sex, nevertheless had to subsist on the same starvation diet.

"Tourists?" the Investigator inquired.

"You must be joking!" the Server replied. "Them, Tourists? Have you taken a good look at them? Have you got a whiff of them?"

"Please, not so loud, they could hear you!" the Investigator murmured.

"They can't understand us, they're not from here. I don't know what language they speak, but it's not ours, that's for sure. They're Displacees."

"Displacees?"

"Yes, Displacees!" And when the Investigator seemed surprised, the Server took it upon himself to add, "What planet do you live on? For several months now, they've been getting turned away in droves, but they keep coming back, and there are always more of them. Have you noticed how many children those women put out? If we could avoid having anything to do with them, we would, but the Hotel is requisitioned by the Repatriation Service, practically every other day. Look at them. Do you think they're unhappy? They're just different, that's all. I hate difference. And I love disinfectants. Take yourself, for example: You smell particularly good, so I'm favorably inclined toward you. Anyway, I was able to save you a table—it's right over there. Management has asked me to express their deep regrets for exposing you to this unseemly spectacle and this disagreeable odor. I'll be back in a moment with your breakfast."

The Investigator walked over to the table the Server had indicated. Its four chairs were all empty. The other tables in the room, several of them only a few steps away, were occupied by large families, by men, women, and children pressed against one another in the greatest discomfort; the Investigator's table, however, was like a protected reserve, a forbidden island. At the other tables, an average of twenty persons huddled wretchedly in an amount of space equivalent to what he had all to himself. Without looking around too much, the Investigator sat down, lowered his head, and waited.

He tried in vain to remember ever having heard of this phenomenon. "Displacees"? Of course, he knew that certain movements of populations were part of reality, and he was aware of the attraction his continent held for a great many individuals. But Displacees?

"Room 93?"

The Investigator didn't have leisure for further reflection. The two Servers standing before him had spoken his room number in unison. He nodded, and with a single motion, the Servers placed two large trays on the table, wished that he would enjoy his meal, and disappeared into the Crowd, which opened a passage for them with some difficulty and very quickly closed up again, like two hands trying to keep their warmth in the hollow of their palms.

XXX

F OUR THICK SLICES OF BACON, three white sausages, two
andouillettes with herbs, a ham omelet, four boiled eggs,
six herring fillets marinated in vinegar and onions, some
small gherkins in sweet-and-sour sauce, smoked salmon
sprinkled with dill, reindeer meatballs, a jar of rillettes,
an assortment of cheeses, a basket of Viennese-style baked
goods, half a pound of butter, grilled toast, aniseed bread,
poppy-seed bread, sesame-seed bread, honey, quince marma-
lade, rose jam, a slice of cheesecake, a pitcher of apple juice, a
bowl of fresh fruit salad, some bananas, some peaches, some
strawberries, a pineapple, five kiwis, a large pot of smoked
black tea, and another of bergamot tea. Not a rusk in sight!
Not a drop of vile black coffee! The Investigator couldn't
believe his eyes. So many delights, and all of them on the
table in front of *him,* the empty-bellied starveling. His head
spun at the sight of all that food, and his dizziness felt like
intoxication. He didn't know where to start, but he knew
he had to, especially since he was afraid the Servers would
change their minds or realize they'd made a mistake and
come back for the trays.

He flung himself on the croissants, the omelet, the herbed
sausages, the poppy-seed bread, cramming the food into his

mouth with his fingers, barely chewing, swallowing things whole, gasping for air; he poured himself cups of steaming tea and drank them down in one gulp, thrust his fingers into the honey, tore apart a herring fillet spread with quince jelly, dunked a chocolate puff pastry into the rillettes jar, mopped up the herring marinade with bacon, wiped his lips with a slice of toast, which he then shoved into his mouth, chewed up and swallowed two bananas at once, nibbled on a reindeer meatball. He felt his belly filling up like a granary after the harvest. He smiled as he devoured, stuffing himself without stint, his head lowered to the bowls, the plates, the cups, abandoning all dignity, not caring in the slightest about the various sauces running down his chin or the stains on his sweater or the state of his fingers, which had been reduced to greasy tongs. And to think how hungry he'd been, so hungry he could have wept. A distant memory. He smiled as he gorged.

"Is everything all right?"

The first Server had just reappeared. At the sound of his voice, the Investigator raised his eyes. "Everything's fine," he said, gesturing at the carnage he'd already perpetrated on the contents of the two trays.

"If there's anything you want, don't hesitate to let us know," the Server said. "That's why we're here."

He bowed, turned, elbowed, and disappeared behind the screen of bodies massed around the Investigator's table. Now only a few inches away from him, they formed a human wall, a compact masonry of eyes, hands, mouths, faces pressed against one another, a living mural of Displacees, observing him, imploring him. He was surrounded by old people and young people, women and men, children and adolescents, crowded next to one another, on top of one another, in thickly serried ranks, in three or four superimposed layers, like a mass grave for the living, and they looked at him, and their wide-open, staring eyes expressed their atrocious hunger, their longing to eat—perhaps even their willingness to kill for—a piece of bread, a slice of sausage, a disk of hard-boiled egg.

The person closest to him was a child. It might have been four or five, or maybe even ten, but it was so thin that it seemed beyond age. The Child—a little human being, scarcely alive, in fact almost dead, its grotesquely distended stomach touching the edge of the table where the food was piled—looked at the Investigator. It didn't ask for anything. It merely looked at the Investigator with its empty eyes. It looked at him from the depths of its exile. It was no longer simply a Displacee. It was also a Witness.

The Investigator dropped the piece of sausage he was still holding between his fingers. No more room. Only with difficulty could he swallow what was in his mouth. His stomach hurt. He was suffocating. Those people were all so close to him. Too close to him. He couldn't get any air. And the Child was staring at him. So were all the others, but the Child most of all, and there was something in its pupils that scored the Investigator's soul like an engraver's tool on a copper plate, and what that tool etched there were questions. Interrogations.

All sounds had ceased. The Investigator undid the big napkin he'd knotted around his neck and dropped it on the table, which was still laden with food. Then, slowly, he got up.

And to think, everything had started off so well.

Little by little, the massed Displacees gave way before the Investigator, as people do before gods or lepers. Just as he was stepping through the door, he met one of the Servers, who asked, "Are you leaving us already?" The Investigator made no reply; he held his belly with both hands and clenched his teeth. He felt like vomiting, but he sensed that he'd never be able to disgorge everything, to eject everything. Because you can never eject everything, he thought. Never. Just as he doubted that one could live happily somewhere without stealing the happiness of someone who lived somewhere else. He shivered. He felt as heavy as a manhole cover, the rubber boot was chafing his boiled foot, and, to top it all, there he was, turning into a philosopher. A pedestrian, banal philosopher, without breadth or depth, wearing a pair of women's panties under apple-green sweatpants, and trotting out pedestrian thoughts, as worn out as old pots tired of always cooking the same soups.

XXXI

S OMEONE WAS DRUMMING on the door of the restroom he'd shut himself up in.

He'd had barely enough time to flee the breakfast room, cross the lobby, spot a door he'd never noticed before—the sign on it read "Men"—plunge through it, and vomit everything he'd just eaten. Now, though the heaving had finally subsided, he was still on all fours with his head half inside the toilet bowl, and the drumming on the door was getting louder.

"I'm coming . . ." he managed to gasp. His voice echoed as though in a cave. He rose regretfully to his feet, wiped his mouth with toilet paper, and unlatched the door.

"Well, I never!" The Policeman was standing in front of him. Attired in a mauve smock with white polka dots, he was holding a long-handled scrub brush in one hand and in the other the blue bucket, which was filled with sponges and cleaning products.

"I'm sorry, I wasn't feeling very well . . ." the Investigator said with a moan.

The Policeman scrutinized his outfit but made no remark.

"I haven't damaged anything, don't worry. Or soiled anything, either. Take a look for yourself."

The Policeman's face suddenly hardened. "I've made no accusations. I was worried about you. I saw you charge into the restroom while I was busy finishing a report—I had my office door ajar, it's too stuffy in there—and you treat me as if I were acting in the line of duty. What do you take me for? Do you think you're the only one who cares about others' misfortunes? Can you believe that the Displacees' pitiful psychological and hygienic conditions don't concern me as much as they do you? I may be the Policeman, but that doesn't make me any less a human being. And even if I don't vomit up my breakfast as you do, their fate nonetheless touches me, and I do everything in my power to make their Displacement as transitory as possible. I try to ensure that, within a very short time, they return to their own proper place, which they should never have left. Now please stand aside, I have work to do."

The Investigator was still going over in his mind what the Policeman had just said, but the latter, his hands protected by a pair of pink rubber gloves, vigorously sprinkled a yellow liquid redolent of bleach and pine resin on the toilet and then, using a sponge, scrubbed the porcelain bowl with all his might.

"You're not a policeman. This isn't a luxury hotel. This is not reality. I'm in a novel, or a dream, and, what's more, probably not in one of my own dreams but in another's dream, the dream of a complex, perverse being having fun at my expense."

The Policeman stood upright, gazed at the Investigator,

seemed to reflect, and in the end dropped the sponge into the bucket. This act produced a strange sound, like a brief sob. Keeping his eyes on the Investigator, the Policeman slowly stripped off his gloves. Then he said, "Follow me."

He said it without violence, almost gently. The Investigator, still surprised by the words that had come out of his own mouth and the tone in which he'd spoken them, was on the verge of apologizing, but he opted instead to remain silent and followed the other's lead.

The Policeman stopped on the exterior steps of the Hotel and said, "I assume you're getting ready to return to the Enterprise this morning for the purposes of your Investigation?"

It was a morning identical to that of the previous day: soft, caressed by a golden light, and filled with intense human activity. A concentrated, compact Crowd surged along the sidewalks on either side of the street, and the roadway was invisible under a flood of vehicles, packed closely together and rolling past at an extremely reduced speed. None of the drivers appeared to be complaining about the slowness of their progress.

"Mild in the morning, ferocious in the evening."

"I beg your pardon?"

"I'm speaking of the climate," the Policeman explained. "At first, I was a little surprised, like you. It didn't make any sense. During the first part of the day, the air is springlike, even summery, but inevitably, toward the end of the afternoon, there's snow, followed in the evening hours by a frost that chews up your face, and then, to cap things off, down comes the night, too soon, falling like a guillotine blade.

That could be a metaphor for life, but I'm not the Poet, I'm the Policeman.

"You pay too much attention to appearances. I really wonder how you can conduct an Investigation of any sort with so little discernment. You see me wearing a housekeeper's smock and carrying a brush, and you jump to premature conclusions. Because my temporary office looks like a broom closet, you tell yourself I'm a simple cleaning person who's lost his mind. No, don't protest! According to what I've been told, that's just what you thought. What a lack of imagination on your part! I could have taken offense. I could have arrested you on the spot—you've given me any number of reasons for doing that, ever since yesterday morning. I could have exercised my arbitrary, limitless power and subjected you to torture of one kind or another, but I believe in the virtues of pedagogy. Come with me."

The Policeman crossed the sidewalk with the most breathtaking ease. The Crowd instantaneously divided into two separate floods. Men and women moved out of his way as he approached, colliding with one another to let him through. No one even grazed him. He reached the curb effortlessly and turned around to assess the Investigator's reaction.

His mouth agape, the Investigator was staring as though he'd just witnessed a miracle. Observing this, the Policeman shrugged his shoulders and smiled, as if to say that the Investigator hadn't seen anything yet. Then he turned toward the street, simply raising one arm and, at the same time, placing his left foot on the asphalt roadway. All the vehicles stopped at once. The sight was astonishing. It was as if a sea had abruptly parted, revealing its rocky bottom—in this case, ordinary blacktop, with ruts or potholes here and there—and forcing its waters to one side or the other. The Policeman crossed the street in a few seconds and stepped onto the opposite sidewalk. There, too, the Crowd took the greatest care to avoid him.

"Do you need any more proof that I'm really the Policeman?" he called out to the Investigator, but the latter was too stunned to reply. His brain was becoming some kind of dwarf mammal, shut up in a wheel and turning it from the inside at top speed, but not producing anything except gratuitous, meaningless, unnecessary motion, along with serious overheating.

"Come on over!" the Policeman cried.

Like an automaton, the Investigator obeyed, crossing the sidewalk and then the street under the mute protection of the Policeman, who oversaw the operation while holding vehicles and pedestrians, still unmoving, under his placid authority. When the Investigator reached the Policeman's side, he set the traffic in motion again with a simple snap of his fingers. With bowed head and shame in his heart, the Investigator remained close to him. Then, after a silence that lasted an eternity, he sheepishly murmured, "Please forgive me."

XXXII

Y OU'RE NOT THE FIRST to be fooled. Before, of course, it
was different; things were clear. But I'm not a man who
regrets the past," the Policeman concluded magnani-
mously, shaking hands with the Investigator. This made him
feel even more ashamed, and he lowered his eyes and said, "I
have a confession to make."

"Come, come, I've already told you that I—"

"It's important to me," the Investigator said, cutting him
off. "I need to confess: This morning, I trashed my room. I
wrecked it. I broke everything. I don't know what got into
me. It was stronger than I was, or, rather, I wasn't myself. I'm
shy and mild-mannered by nature, but this morning I turned
into a monster, a savage beast. When I think back on it, I
believe I would have been capable of killing someone."

He kept his eyes fixed on the floor. He was prepared to
put up with a long interrogation, a re-enactment, perhaps
prolonged standing at attention, but the Policeman's reaction was immediately good-natured: "Come on, you're too
hard on yourself! Killing! The things you say! My profession
has taught me that killing's not easy. It's not something just
anybody can do. And I don't want to offend you, but you don't
have what it takes to be a murderer. You haven't been desig-

nated as the Investigator for nothing. You weren't considered qualified to be the Killer. Stick to your proper job. As for your room, don't give it another thought! My people showed it to me while you were having breakfast. Now, it's true you went at it pretty vigorously, but you were right to do so! The room was unworthy of you. The person responsible is the one who dared to assign you to that room. Nobody's going to quibble with you about a little breakage! Case closed! Moreover, I've already filed my report, and the Guilty Party shall pay, I can guarantee you that!"

"But who is the Guilty Party?"

"I'm looking into that. I'll find him. And if I don't find him, I'll invent him. I'm formidable in my field. I forbid you to concern yourself for a single second with anything more than this: You have a very important mission to carry out. You're the Investigator."

The two of them had arrived in front of the Guardhouse. The Policeman, who had insisted on accompanying the Investigator there, pressed the buzzer himself and spoke to the Guard. Was he the same one as the previous morning? If there were two of them, they were physically identical. The Policeman advised the Guard to treat the Investigator well. "He's a friend," the Policeman said meaningfully.

Friendship is a rare thing, and the Investigator had never tried it. Many human beings go through life without ever experiencing friendship, and some miss out on love, too, whereas it's a banal, frequent, and daily occurrence for them to feel indifference, anger, or hatred, and to be motivated by envy, jealousy, or the spirit of revenge. The Investigator wondered whether the Policeman really felt the emotions he was expressing. Were his words merely formulaic? When the polka-dot smock disappeared in the Crowd, the Investigator was still standing in front of the Guardhouse; the fingers of his right hand stroked the medicine bottle that contained the new tablets his friend had given him in parting.

The Guard was waiting, smiling at him from behind the glass partition. The Investigator turned to him, moved his head in the direction the Policeman had taken, and heard himself say, "He's a friend." As he pronounced these words, the Investigator felt a pleasant stirring begin in his belly and rise gradually, in little waves, to his heart and lungs, and thence to his soul. "I'm sorry, but my identification documents still haven't been returned to me," he went on.

"No problem," the Guard replied. "You're the Policeman's friend. I'll call the Guide. Would you please be so kind as to direct your steps toward the entrance?"

The Investigator told himself that everything was decidedly looking up on this new morning. The sun was doing the sun's job. The weather was fine. The behavior of all the persons he'd talked to had been strictly normal. I can even hear birds singing, he thought. The world is in its proper place and going round as it should.

Less than an hour earlier, the Investigator had been devouring pounds of food under the eyes of famished, frightened, exiled human beings about to be sent back to the wretchedness they'd run from. Then, seized by a sense of guilt and shame he could neither master nor ignore, he'd violently vomited everything he'd eaten. So weak and disoriented had he been that he'd called into doubt the very existence of the universe he was moving in and the materiality of the people he was encountering. But a problem-free street crossing, a friendly word spoken by a man, the Policeman, whom to all intents and purposes he barely knew, a smile from a minor functionary separated from him by a glass partition, a ray of sunlight, and an air of spring had sufficed to make him forget the sufferings of others, his own confusion, his fever, his aching forehead, his solitude, his Investigation, and even his hunger. The Investigator was trying his hand at forgetting, which keeps many people from dying too soon.

The Security Officer came out to meet him and, there could be no doubt, he was surely the same one as the day before. The realization dealt a blow to the Investigator's good humor. The memory of this muscle-bound fellow's arrogant indifference tarnished the young day's early light.

"Had a good night? Slept well?"

The Security Officer was still two heads taller than the Investigator. As before, he was wearing a perfectly crisp paramilitary uniform, and the same tools for communications, attack, and defense were hanging from his belt, but he was looking at the Investigator with great benevolence, his mouth open in a smile whose whiteness was practically supernatural.

"I must have seemed a bit harsh to you yesterday," the Security Officer said. "But what can you expect? That's my job. Yours is to investigate, and mine is to be on the lookout. And no one's going to take me seriously as a vigilant sentry unless I put on a surly face and a whole array of knickknacks"—his broad hands indicated all the things dangling from his belt—"which, by the way, are totally useless. I spend my on-duty time silencing my feelings, disguising them, nipping them in the bud, even though yesterday, for example, all I wanted to do was to give you a hug."

"Give me . . . a hug?" the Investigator stammered.

"You didn't notice a thing, right? I don't mean to boast, but I'm a good actor. I thought about it all night long. I was cross with myself for not having done it. Regrets are terrible. My life is loaded with regrets, and it's getting harder and harder for me to live with them. I look into other people's eyes, and I see what I am to them: a uniform, a brutish type doing a brutish job. They stare at me as if I were an animal, a mound of muscles, a beast without a brain. But I have a brain, and above all, I have a heart. A beating heart, a heart that needs love. Do you know, at night, when I take off this uniform and these doodads, when I'm naked and alone again, I weep? Like a child who's been punished or abandoned. When I saw you yesterday, I felt you could understand me. I felt you were like me, and that we were two of a kind. I wasn't mistaken, was I?"

The Investigator was dumbstruck.

"Tell me, was I mistaken?" the Security Officer repeated imploringly.

The Investigator made a vague gesture that might have passed for encouraging.

"I was sure I was right. I vowed last night that if the situation arose again, I wouldn't cause myself any additional regrets. And so, if you have no objections, I'd love to give you a hug, right here, right now. It's not every day that one has the good fortune to meet an investigator, to say nothing of *the* Investigator, a man who plays a leading role, whereas I, I'm a mere underling, a shadowy figure summoned at the last minute and very quickly forgotten, a secondary character. It's my lot in life. A fate I've grown used to. I accept it."

Basically, the Investigator said to himself, this could be just another form of torture. The extravagant benevolence and the exaggerated friendliness, both of them unmotivated and ridiculously hyperbolic, were of a piece with the rest: the brutality, the mistreatment, the indifference, the nitpicking, the absurdity. This is another test, he thought. I'm being messed with. I'm being studied. I'm nothing but a toy, undergoing performance evaluations before being put on the market. Surely someone, somewhere, is watching me. But who? My boss, the Head of Section? His boss? His boss's boss? The Manager? The Guide who is also the Watchman? The Policeman who claims to be my friend? The Giantess who rules the Hotel? God? Someone more important than God? All my reactions are being noted. I'm probably in the midst of some sort of validation protocol, some convoluted quality-control process, under observation by an entire team of men in white, Scientists, Censors, Judges, Arbiters, and who knows what else. I'm supposed to be the Investigator, but am I not myself the center of another Investigation, one that goes well beyond me, one whose stakes are much more vital than those of the one I'm conducting?

"Well?" said the Security Officer ecstatically.

"Well, what?"

"May I give you a hug?"

This was a strange scene indeed, though nobody saw it: the huge Security Officer, with his Minotaur's forehead, clutching the puny Investigator to his bosom, wrapping his immense arms around him, holding him tight for a long moment, almost smothering him, as though desperately trying to experience the living character of another individual homologous to himself, yearning to feel a sense of belonging to the same species, seeking the certitude of being chained to the same bench in the same galley.

The embrace was ended by a crackling sound in the Security Officer's earpiece. As though he'd been called to order, he released the Investigator at once and took two steps backward, his face hard and serious again. He listened. And the Investigator, who'd been on the verge of suffocation, was finally able to breathe.

The caller spoke to the Security Officer at length. Something was being explained to him. He responded from time to time, always in the same manner, repeating the word "Affirmative" or the expression "I read you loud and clear," putting them in play alternately, as a juggler does with balls or tenpins.

He towered over the Investigator, and it occurred to the latter that, of all the people he'd spoken to, only this man was so tall, so powerfully built, so young, so thick-haired; the others conformed to the same physical type—pretty short, pretty bald, pretty middle-aged—as he, the Investigator, did. This observation was of no use to him. Men often have thoughts whose immediate utility they don't see, and besides, many of the said thoughts turn out to have no usefulness at all. But thinking is sometimes like running an empty washing machine: The exercise may serve to verify proper functioning, but the dirty laundry left outside the machine stays dirty eternally.

XXXIII

THE INVESTIGATOR WAS FOLLOWING the green line. He was doing what the Security Officer had told him to do, and the Security Officer had told him to do what he'd been told to tell him. Thus far, everything was clear. Someone had made a decision and that decision had been put into force, as witnessed by the Investigator's scrupulous adherence to the indicated path. He stepped meticulously, one foot after the other, and neither foot ever deviated from the green line. The ribbon of color he trod had materialized on the ground at some time in the past, produced by a man who'd been given the mission to paint that ribbon and had carried out his task without trying to understand why it had been assigned to him or what good it served.

The Investigator walked on. He didn't know where he was headed, but that didn't worry him. He'd poured out the tablets from the new medicine bottle his friend the Policeman had given him and popped them all into his mouth at once. He chewed them with relish, savoring their bitterness and their subtle bouquet of medicinal plants.

He was thinking kindly thoughts about the Policeman and the Security Officer, and also about the Guide, who according to the Security Officer—there again, he'd been told to tell him—had fallen victim to a Level 6 Impediment and would be unable to receive the Investigator that morning. When the Investigator asked the Security Officer what a Level 6 Impediment was, the other replied that he hadn't the least idea, and that it didn't lie within the parameters of his function to possess such information; his mission was limited to ensuring that no unauthorized visitor penetrated inside the walls of the Enterprise. Order doesn't exist without the concept of society. People often think the reverse, but they're wrong. Man created order at a time when nothing was required of him. He thought himself clever. He's had cause to regret it.

Walking along at a moderate pace, the Investigator let strange theoretical analyses occupy his mind. A group of thirty-seven people—eleven women and twenty-six men, all Asians—overtook and passed him. Wearing hard hats and white coats and "External Element" badges, they were following the red line at a rapid clip. He envied them. Not because they were following the red line, but because of the hard hats and the coats. He missed them. The long white coat would have at least allowed him to hide his apple-green sweatpants and mended raincoat, and the hard hat would have given him a serious, professional air, which he thought he no longer had. But the Security Officer could do nothing for him in this regard, having in his possession neither a white coat nor a hard hat. It was the Guides' job to provide External Elements with those items.

By now, the Asian group was nothing but a memory on the horizon. The Investigator continued to follow the green line. He appreciated having a goal. His cold was getting better, even if his scarlet, swollen nose, an organ worthy of a clown, remained painful, as did his boiled foot, chafed by the rubber boot he was wearing, and the wound on his forehead, which was beginning to close, thanks to a sort of brownish crust whose design recalled a bishop's crosier or a scorpion's tail.

The Investigator strolled along languidly, like an idler. He wouldn't have looked out of place loitering in a landscape on a Sunday afternoon in October, on the banks of a canal decorated with a luminous fog whose densest parts, as compact as flax tows, clung to the blond branches of old poplars.

But his tranquil gait was deceiving; in fact, the Investigator didn't miss any of what he saw around him. He had the feeling that his vision had become sharper, and that all his senses were in a heightened state of awareness. The thought of beginning his Investigation acted like a stimulating drug. His body, with its modest proportions, feeble muscles, and consummate flabbiness, seemed reinvigorated, newly energetic. He was going into action. He was becoming himself again.

Mentally, the Investigator recorded every building he passed close to. With subtle details and remarkable scope as far as the overall layout of the place was concerned, he successfully reconstructed in his head, as he walked along, a three-dimensional model of the part of the Enterprise he could see. It was by no means certain that this exercise would prove to be of much use in the Investigator's future, but at least it demonstrated his ability to disengage from direct, material contingencies in order to conceive a schematized idea of physical structures that employed different materials—molybdenum, mild steels, photovoltaic panels— and had been constructed at various times.

What was happening to him? Why all these thoughts? They weren't like him, none of them. What voice was speaking inside his skull? He stopped. He was dripping with sweat. He recalled his Section Accountant and remembered having once heard her speaking to a Secretary about the voices she, the Accountant, heard from time to time, voices that told her to do this or that, to wear black patent pumps on Fridays, to eat chicken three times a week, to run through the public gardens humming a current hit tune, to lean against her balcony railing and show her naked bosom to the old man in the opposite apartment. Hidden behind the coffee machine, the Investigator had been staggered by her words.

Could it be that he, too, was the victim of inner voices? He pricked up his ears, but he couldn't hear a thing except the humming of the Enterprise, a sort of one-note music, like the sound of an electrical transformer. However, all those thoughts he couldn't get rid of, the vocabulary that kept invading his mind in successive waves—they were none of them his. And what if someone—something?—were insidiously beginning to inhabit him, entering his brain and his body, his movements and his words? How, under those conditions, was he supposed to become himself again, despite what he'd thought a few minutes before?

The Investigator compelled himself to stop thinking. He gradually quickened his pace, staring at the green line as if it were the guarantee of his salvation. Then he was almost running, his eyes still fixed on the ribbon of green, the ribbon that represented the course of his life and his destiny, the ribbon he looked upon as an indispensable tool, a safeguard. He started going even faster, his heart pounding in his chest, his breath growing short, sweat dripping from his forehead, down his back, between his shoulder blades, under his armpits, down the back of his neck. Running now, faster and faster, running till he thought his lungs would burst, running as if his life depended on it, he kept his eyes riveted on the green line. The green line replaced all thought. The green line sucked up his gray matter, kneaded it, made it change color, gave it tonalities of celadon, jade, emerald, olive green, forest green.

The shock was extremely violent. The Investigator, with lowered head, sprinting along at maximum speed, galvanized by the tablets given him by his friend the Policeman, crashed head-on, without any last-second attempt to slow his momentum, into a wall of large cement blocks, at the foot of which the green line ended its horizontal run. He lay stretched out on the ground, released from consciousness. His body was relaxed. His cerebral activity was suspended. A swelling like a pigeon's egg appeared on his forehead, exactly where he'd cut himself before; the wound had reopened, and a thin stream of dark blood was flowing from it.

The temperature started dropping; the sky darkened. Heavy clouds, like enormous, laden barges apparently gathering for a rendezvous, came rolling in from all sides, driven by disgruntled winds. It wasn't long before the clouds began to bump into one another, smash into one another, rip one another open; and the first drops of icy rain fell on the Investigator, who lay there, still unconscious, and didn't even feel them.

XXXIV

URING THOSE SEVERAL HOURS, the ones he spent lying
unconscious on the ground, the Investigator's assessment
of things was accurate; he was indeed dreaming. His
was a real dream, that is to say, a mental construction produced when the mind is at rest, when it has no other employ-
ment, when it's slothful and seeks none, when it's curled up
in idleness and refuses all offers of activity. The nonsense
that informs the content of most real dreams is an allegorical
testimony to the pernicious consequences the absence of work
can have for every individual.

The Investigator passed the Enterprise's Suicides in
review. They'd all been brought into a room and lined up
on the floor, one next to the other: twenty-two bodies plus
one urn, containing the ashes of an employee who'd been
cremated.

The Suicides still bore the signs of their final actions.
Seven had ropes around their necks and protruding tongues.
Six presented temples shattered by single pistol shots. One's
throat was slit; for three others, it was the veins in their
wrists; two more had charred bodies, the result of their
self-immolation; another's totally cyanotic face was visible

through the plastic bag he'd used to smother himself; water dripped from the bodies of two who had leaped into the river.

They were all resolutely dead, there was no doubt about it, and yet the eyes of each followed the Investigator as he moved from one to another, studying them minutely and professionally. That vision, which might well have frightened him, didn't disturb him in the least. Similarly, he found it completely normal that the Suicides answered all the questions he put to them concerning the procedures they'd followed, their motivations, whether their successful effort had been preceded by one or more previous attempts, and the reasons why those attempts had failed. Thus far, the Investigator had somewhat neglected the urn, but when he asked who had died from gas, it was the urn that replied, and the fact that a funeral urn began to speak didn't strike him as the least bit absurd.

"It was me, sir," it said.

"Please call me 'Mr. Investigator.'"

"Very well, Mr. Investigator."

"So the gas, that's you?"

"Yes."

"One question comes to mind: Was it an accident, or was it suicide?"

"A little of both, Mr. Investigator."

"What do you mean? That's impossible."

The urn seemed to hesitate before speaking again.

"I had the intention of committing suicide. My mind was made up. But I wanted to throw myself from a window, and I didn't have time to do that. The explosion happened just as I was about to jump."

"Were you in your apartment?"

"Yes. I'd made some coffee to give myself courage. I must have turned off the burner but forgotten to close the gas valve. It took me a long time to take the plunge, if I may use the expression. The gas escaped. I didn't smell anything—my nose was always stopped up, owing to my numerous allergies, notably to hazel and birch pollen, acarids, and cat hair, allergies that had poisoned my existence ever since adolescence. I climbed up on the windowsill, turned the catch, and then boom. After that, nothing."

"Boom?"

"Yes, boom, Mr. Investigator. A great boom. It's the last memory I carry from the world of the living."

The Investigator reflected a few moments, contemplated the urn at length, and noticed that all the other Suicides were attentively following the conversation, doubtless waiting to learn what his conclusion would be.

"Well," the Investigator said, "that makes no difference, because you wanted to kill yourself and now you're dead."

"At the risk of taking up too much of your time, and with your permission, I'm not completely in agreement with you, Mr. Investigator," the urn said hesitantly. "I'm certainly dead, but my death didn't occur at all the way I wanted it to. And may I point out that I died several seconds before I was able to kill myself? Therefore, it wasn't really suicide."

"But you fell from the window all the same, didn't you?"

Noting the urn's apparent confusion, the Investigator told himself he'd just scored a point.

"Ye-e-es . . ." the urn said. "That's undeniable, but . . . what actually caused my death? The fall? A cardiac arrest resulting from the shock and terror of the explosion? Or the explosion itself, which could have torn apart my lungs and

all my other organs, thus leading to death almost instantaneously, or at least prior to the moment when my head struck
the ground?"

"I'm waiting for you to answer those questions! What was
the cause of death recorded in the autopsy report?"

"There wasn't any autopsy. My wife had me cremated
before the Police or the Enterprise had the time to demand
one."

The Investigator was stunned. All things considered, it
was impossible to determine whether this particular case
was a suicide or an accident. The statistical table he'd wanted
to include in his Investigation made no provisions for such a
scenario, and in the realm of statistics, uncertainty was intolerable. This state of affairs would discredit the seriousness of
his work, and as a result, he himself would be undermined.

The urn remained silent, clearly ill at ease for having put
the Investigator in such an embarrassing predicament. The
Suicides looked away. Everyone could perceive the Investigator's mounting anxiety. The moment was drawn out to such
a length that it seemed it would never end.

He was delivered from it by unbearable pain.

"Don't move! I'll be gentle," said a voice. A woman was
bending over him. He hadn't seen her before, yet she looked
familiar to him. She had a round face, unmarked by age, and
fine hair. She was wearing a long white coat. By all indica-
tions, she was either a nurse or a physician.

"What happened to me?" asked the Investigator, brutally
yanked out of his dream. In every part of his skull, he felt
rare, concentrated, excruciating pain.

"You ran into the wall. It happens often enough when
people are distracted. Most of them get away with a bump,

but I figure you must have been running like the wind if you put yourself in this state. When you were picked up, you were completely unconscious. Still, you were luckier than the Korean."

"What Korean?"

"Two months ago. But he must have been moving even faster than you were—those people put a great deal of energy into whatever they do. That's what gives them their economic force. The result was a Level 7 Impediment."

"And that is . . . ?"

"Death," the woman replied distractedly, injecting some substance into the Investigator's arm as she spoke.

"I was only following the line . . ." the Investigator murmured, as if to himself. He was thinking about the faceless Korean, whose fate the Investigator had just barely escaped.

"The problem," the woman went on, "is that everyone follows that line without exercising good judgment. If you raise your eyes, you see quite clearly that the line goes straight into a wall. It's the result of bad planning or a discreet attempt at sabotage; we'll never know. The Employee who painted the line misunderstood his orders, or maybe he didn't want to understand them, and, rather than make the line veer off to the right so that it would lead people to my office, he let it go smack into the wall and even continued it up the wall, for close to seven feet—that is, to the highest point his brush could reach—and then he finished off the line with an arrowhead pointing to the clouds. Your case, like the Korean's, is extreme, but bear in mind that I've seen certain individuals approach that wall and try to scale it because they didn't want to stray from the green line. They tried to climb that wall, even though it's about sixteen feet high, it offers no handholds, and it's topped by barbed wire. As a result, they cut their fingers and broke their nails, and to go where? To the sky? You can understand the degree of psychological conditioning people have undergone when you observe them in certain circumstances, like when they're supposed to obey instructions, advice, or orders."

This whole conversation was still a little complex for the Investigator, whose badly bruised head had allowed him to grasp some fragments—the line into the wall, the Korean's death, Level 7 Impediments—and not others, which were too abstruse for him at that moment. "How would you assess my Impediment level?" he asked.

The woman looked at him, palpated his forehead, which made him cry out in pain, took his pulse, closely examined the whites of his eyes.

"Our Impediment scale goes from Level 1, which consists in absenting oneself from one's work for two minutes to go to the restroom, to Level 7, which designates the irreversible cessation of an individual's bodily functions. After a cursory examination, and with the obvious stipulation that this assessment cannot be used in a claim proceeding before an insurance company or in a court of law within the framework of a judicial action brought against the Enterprise, I'd say that you are the object of a Level 3 Impediment, but that, I repeat, is not an actual diagnosis. Certain skull fractures, for example, are undetectable in a superficial examination, but that doesn't stop them from causing a swift death a few hours later."

The Investigator's thoughts turned to the Guide, who the Security Officer had told him was the victim of a Level 6 Impediment. Wondering what such an Impediment entailed, the Investigator couldn't stop himself from asking the woman to define it.

"Cessation of cerebral function."

The Investigator began to tremble. He felt a knot forming in his throat. What could have happened to the Guide? "Thank you, Doctor," he groaned.

"Please don't think I'm reproaching you for your mistake, but I'm not a doctor, I'm a psychologist," the woman replied with a smile, and as he looked at that smile, it was as if he were contemplating his reflection in a mirror, a reflection of himself with a little lipstick on his lips, lightly made-up eyelids, and rather more hair.

The Psychologist stood up. "I believe you have now recovered sufficiently to follow me. We're going to my office."

XXXV

T HE INVESTIGATOR LET HIMSELF be taken by the arm
and guided like a sick child. They left the room, which
might have been some sort of infirmary. As he walked,
he realized he wasn't wearing his raincoat anymore, or his
sweatpants, either; what he had on was a simple hospital
gown, salmon in color, made of some light, comfortable
material—cotton, maybe Indian cotton, doubtless not silk,
such a precious fabric would never be used in manufacturing
that sort of garment, but the impression it left on the skin
was nevertheless like that left by silk, warm and ethereal—
and reaching down to the middle of his thighs. He had the
awkward feeling that he was totally naked under the gown,
but he didn't have the nerve to check.

They were stepping warily down a white corridor whose
floor, walls, and ceiling seemed to be covered with foam pad-
ding, which muffled the sounds of their progress and made
walking an activity both delicate and spongy. At the end of
about a hundred yards, the Psychologist opened a door on the
left. He entered and led the Investigator to a swivel chair,
chose for himself a wheeled stool—a rather tall metal object
with a seat shaped like a tractor seat, one of those stools that

hairdressers use to rotate around their clients—and rolled himself very close to the Investigator.

The office décor presented nothing of interest, or in any case nothing sufficiently arresting for one to pause and describe it. Nevertheless, one item leaped to the Investigator's eyes—namely, the immense portrait of the Old Man; the face, clothes, and pose, he saw, were identical to those in the photographs on the key ring, in the Hotel room, and in the Manager's office. Although the Investigator didn't understand why, this realization terrified him, and his disquiet didn't escape the Psychologist's notice.

"Why are you looking at the wall?" he asked.

The panic-stricken Investigator couldn't detach his gaze from the Old Man's smile, from his drooping eyelids, whose curves exactly matched those of his mustache, from the light—mocking? cheerful? kindly? appalling?—that burned in his eyes, from his wrinkled, liver-spotted, fissured hands, by themselves a résumé of great age, or from his clothes, which the viewer felt like stroking, and against which he could perhaps snuggle up and fall asleep, so that thus he might obtain forgiveness for his mistakes, for his lies, for his lesser and greater sins.

"That man there . . ."

"A man? Talk to me about him," the Psychologist said, having just looked at the wall himself.

"I beg your pardon?"

"You mentioned a man. Who is he?"

"I don't know. . . . I don't know. I have a vague notion. . . ."

"If it makes you feel any better, so do we all."

"Is he the Founder?" the Investigator ventured to ask.

Moving like a crab, the Psychologist rolled his stool to one side, placed himself facing the Investigator, and repeated "The Founder?" in a puzzled voice.

"Yes. Is he the Founder?"

The Psychologist hesitated, seemed about to say something, reconsidered, and shrugged. "If you say so! Well, good. Now, provided you have no objection, I'd like us to talk about you. What brings you here?"

The Investigator would have gladly swallowed one or two of his friend the Policeman's blue-and-yellow tablets, but the medicine bottle, like his discharged cell phone, had remained in his raincoat, and in any case, the bottle was empty. He wondered where his clothes could be. He didn't miss them very much; the gown he had on was generally much more practical and certainly much nicer; he thought it becoming, and it was as thin and soft as a second skin.

Forgetting his headache and gathering his thoughts, he began to give a summary of his situation to the Psychologist. He started with his arrival in the City, repeatedly stressed his status and his mission, recounted his wanderings in the streets, his sensation of being lost, of being manipulated, the strangeness of the Hotel, the differences in how he was treated from one morning to the next, the Policeman's hostile and then friendly behavior, the conduct of the Giantess; he talked about the deserted nighttime streets, about his feelings of abandonment and isolation, about the vastness of the Enterprise, which encompassed the entire City and perhaps even the visible world, about the Crowd that inundated the City during the day, impeding the slightest movement, unless you were a policeman, in which case the Crowd became a flock of sheep that a symbolic cudgel blow, a raised hand, a glaring eye sufficed to bring under control, about hostile sandwich-vending machines, about the Exceptional Authorization, about the Manager's unsuccessful leap over his desk, about the Guide who was also the Watchman, about room 93, which the Investigator had methodically trashed, about the Tourists, the Displacees, the inconstancy of the weather, and the inability of the Hotel's Architects to design stair risers of uniform height.

"Have you finished?" the Psychologist asked.

"Yes, I think so. I don't have anything to add, at least not at the moment."

The Investigator had spoken for almost an hour. Talking had done him good. He felt that the Psychologist could understand him. Now the Psychologist got off his wheeled stool and went to sit behind the desk. He opened a drawer and took out an index card and a promotional ballpoint pen on which the Investigator thought he recognized the photograph of the Old Man, but the reproduction was so small that he couldn't be sure. The Psychologist jotted down a few words the Investigator was unable to read.

"Your name, please?" The Psychologist kept his head down and his eyes on the index card, doubtless assuming that the reply to his question would come too quickly to warrant raising his head and looking at the person across the desk.

"My name?"

"Yes."

His head still lowered, the Psychologist was holding his pen ready to write down the Investigator's name; the ballpoint hovered an inch above the card.

"My name . . . my name . . . ?" the Investigator stammered, making an immense effort that he tried to hide behind a smile. In spite of himself, what he produced seemed rather like a grimace.

The Psychologist slowly raised his head and looked across the desk. His face betrayed not the slightest emotion, not the smallest thought inclined this way or that. In other words, it was impossible at that moment to know what the Psychologist thought about the Investigator or about the Investigator's hesitation in giving his name. Only the fact of his having lifted his head, that is, of his having swapped a banal attitude for one a little less so, one that suggested a more intense— more intrigued?—attention, indicated that the time the Investigator was taking to reply to him constituted, in his opinion, an opinion given weight by his status as a clinician and supported by his knowledge and long professional experience (he was not in his first youth), an almost imperceptible break with normality.

Meanwhile, the Investigator was losing his footing, sinking in quicksand, experiencing something whose existence he'd always doubted. For years, he'd filed quicksand in the same mental drawer that contained Aladdin's lamp, flying carpets, Scheherazade's stories, and Sinbad's Cyclops. He'd heard about all those things, but they'd remained hearsay. Legends and stories had never interested him. He did without them. He left all that to children. He was wrong.

"You don't remember your name?"

XXXVI

THE INVESTIGATOR BURST OUT LAUGHING. It was a big laugh, protracted and supple, and he made it last as long as possible, hoping that the Psychologist would find this slightly artificial good humor infectious and join him in modulating to a brighter key. But the longer the laugh went on, the more forced it in fact became; and the harder the Investigator tried to keep it up, to infuse it with new variations, the more rigid the Psychologist's face grew, and the more it changed into a dull, unyielding surface, as cold as a rock, as impenetrable as granite.

The Psychologist placed his pen on the index card, and then the Investigator stopped laughing. He knew he'd lost. His thoughts started to race about in his head, rushing in every direction like creatures trapped in a circular room, dashing around it, charging its walls, crashing into them, rebounding, howling, injuring themselves, calling out, begging for deliverance, or at least for a response. He was searching. He was searching for his name. The name that was written on his identity papers. A simple action would have sufficed, a glance at a little plastic card bearing his photograph with his name printed under it. Could he have forgotten his own name? Was this among the consequences of his accident with the wall? You don't forget your name! He must have said it a dozen times since his arrival in the City. Of course! He thought about that, passed in review all his encounters with other people—they hadn't been so numerous—and tried to remember how he'd presented himself to them. "I'm the Investigator." "Hello, I'm the Investigator." "Let me introduce myself: I'm the Investigator." The sentences followed one after another, all of them identical or nearly so. The Investigator recalled that he always designated himself as the Investigator, which happened to be precisely what he was. But he gave no name. No name at all. Ever.

"I'm the Investigator," he finally said to the Psychologist, raising his shoulders and letting them fall at once by way of apology for the obviousness of his assertion.

The Psychologist stood up, returned to his rolling stool, sat on it, and scooted over to a spot very close to the Investigator. His hard face softened somewhat, and when he began to speak again, his voice was mild.

"Are you aware that you've talked of nothing but functions ever since the beginning of our session? You're the Investigator, and you refer to the Policeman, the Guide, the Watchman, the Server, the Guard, the Manager, the Security Officer, the Founder. You never use proper names, not for yourself or anyone else. Sometimes you add a numerical adornment—you're number 14, you're number 93—but it comes down to the same thing. Answer this simple question: Who am I to you?"

"You're the Psychologist. You told me so."

"No. I told you I was a psychologist, not *the* Psychologist. Besides, you seem not to have noticed that I'm a woman, and your failure to observe this obvious fact confirms my analysis. You deny all humanity, in yourself and in those around you. You see people and the world as an impersonal, asexual system of functions, of cogs and gears, a great mechanism without intelligence in which those functions and cogs operate and interact in order to make it work. When you refer to a group, it's always vague, it has no precise limits. You mention the Enterprise, the Crowd, the Tourists, the Displacees, nebulous entities one doesn't know whether to take literally or metaphorically."

"What about the Giantess?" the Investigator cried, full of hope, as if he'd retrieved the blessed formula for sending an SOS, even though he could feel that his ship was already almost completely submerged.

"The Giantess," the Psychologist repeated, smiling one of those smiles bestowed on a person who's having trouble understanding even though he's been provided with all the elements he needs to understand. "The Giantess is also the Mother, your Mother, as simple as that. Or you might as well have said the Woman. Here again, you designate someone by function, and the exaggeration of the function that can be seen in your use of the word 'Giantess' simply transcribes the oppression you seem to feel when faced with the feminine, and perhaps also the fantasy of being dominated by it, enveloped by it, of returning by a sort of reverse childbirth into the greater, the first, the ancestral womb, as a way of escaping a world in which you find it difficult to win, or to keep, your proper place."

The Giantess, his Mother! His Mother, to whose womb he dreamed of returning. This woman was mad! To prove it, the Investigator couldn't even remember his Mother's face.

"Moreover, this is the reason why you were wearing women's undergarments, isn't it?"

"I beg your pardon?"

The Psychologist rolled his stool over to a small cabinet, opened one of its drawers, thrust his hand inside, and pulled out the pink panties with the black lace trim. He waved this article of clothing in the air for a few seconds before letting it drop back into the drawer, which he closed with a flick of his fingers.

"I can explain everything . . ." stammered the humiliated Investigator.

"But I'm not asking you for any explanation. I'm not the Policeman, to use your terminology. It's *my* job to furnish explanations, that's what *I'm* paid to do, not you. Since you respect functions so much, I ask you please not to confuse them, but, rather, tell me about this famous Investigation of yours. Who sent you on this mission?"

"The Head of Section," the Investigator answered quickly, glad to let the little pair of panties lie forgotten in the Psychologist's drawer.

"Once again, you're identifying someone in terms of his function. What's his name?"

"I don't know. I have no idea! Among ourselves, we always call him the Head of Section. He's the Head of Section, and that's it."

"When you say 'Among ourselves,' to whom are you referring?"

"Well, the others! The other Investigators!"

"There are several of you?"

"Yes."

"How many?"

"I don't know the answer to that! Five, six, a dozen, hundreds, or even more, I have no idea. The Head of Section knows. It's not my job to know!"

"And if I ask you the names of some of the other Investigators, you'll say . . ."

"I don't know their names. I run into them infrequently, I never speak to them, I stay focused on my Investigations."

The conversation was turning into torture. The Investigator kept getting bogged down in responses that weren't responses at all. His awareness of this fact had the effect of making him feel even more fragile, and to top it all, he saw the Psychologist's eyes change and read there the progressive metamorphosis taking place in the professional's mind. Little by little, the Psychologist was ceasing to consider the Investigator a person somewhat like himself, a person evolving in a relatively normal fashion, though understandably given to some perversions and foibles that were, on the whole, socially and humanly acceptable, and now he was beginning, little by little, to apprehend the Investigator in all his difference, a difference that was obviously pathological, monstrous, a unique case whose study would prove to be, if not exciting, at least completely odd.

"And this Investigation, let's talk about it. Its object is supposed to be . . . ?" the Psychologist replied, letting his words fly through the air and hang there suspended.

"The Suicides."

"The Suicides?"

"Yes, the epidemic of Suicides that has struck the Enterprise over the course of the past several months."

"I'm not familiar with them, and if there's anyone who should know about such matters, it's me. Do you have proof of what you're saying?"

"My Head of Section isn't in the habit of playing jokes. He has a horror of wasting his time and making his subordinates waste theirs. I have to suppose that if he sent me here to this City to investigate a wave of suicides inside the Enterprise, then that wave exists. And besides—even though I think this is going to make you smile, I'm going to say it anyway, because I've reached the point where I no longer have any-thing left to lose, and certainly not face—I met the Suicides in a dream, and I was able to talk to them. It was right after I ran into the wall."

The Psychologist took a deep breath, smiled, lifted his arms skyward, and let them fall back to his thighs. "Natu-rally!" he said.

He put his right hand on the Investigator's shoulder and patted it a little. It was a slumped, soft shoulder, a shoulder one would have thought had no bones to support it, nothing but fat and atrophied muscles; and it formed part of a mal-treated body that had eaten nothing for three days.

"You've convinced me," the Psychologist said. "I'm going to do everything in my power to ensure that you'll be able to bring your Investigation to a successful conclusion."

He returned to his desk and wrote a long letter. "A sort of 'open sesame' to help you get through doors," he said. From time to time as he wrote, he would look up and give the Investigator a kindly glance.

Finally feeling reassured, the Investigator was able to relax. He considered himself very close to starting work on his mission in earnest. His confidence returned, and this feeling wasn't due solely to the comfortable fabric of his thin hospital gown—he ran his fingers over it, first in one direction and then in another, using a slow, caressing motion—or even to the Policeman's medicine. This temporary fragment of happiness arose from the conclusion he'd come to: You should always play with all your cards on the table, he told himself, it's the only way to be taken seriously in life, even if the cards sometimes present unseemly figures, blind kings, one-eyed jacks, questionable queens, which can disconcert the strongest among us and make them mistrust the hand they've been dealt. Fortunately, however, there are individuals who think beyond appearances. And the Investigator, while reflecting upon all those things, admired the features of the Psychologist, bent over his desk, as we admire the men and women who comfort us in our existence.

XXXVII

THE PSYCHOLOGIST HAD SEALED the envelope, and it wouldn't have occurred to the Investigator to open the letter and read it, because the Psychologist had addressed the envelope in such a way that the bearer was simultaneously comforted and interdicted from looking inside. The large capital letters, written in a self-assured hand that brooked no opposition and contained no trace of hesitation, read: TO THE FOUNDER.

The Investigator was sitting in a sort of waiting room. The Psychologist had led him there, very kindly assisting his every step along the way, as if he were quite ill, when in reality—if he excepted the pain still drilling inside his head, and even that was beginning to abate—his general condition seemed to him to be pretty satisfactory. His hunger had stopped tormenting him, and he wasn't even thirsty.

"Take a seat," the Psychologist had said. "I'm going to look for, I'm going to look for . . . ah, what should I call them? Something you'd like . . ." He'd hesitated a moment with his left index finger on his lips as he contemplated the Investigator. "How about 'Escorts'? Would that be all right with you, Escorts?"

"Escorts? But that's perfect!" the Investigator had seen fit to reply. The very term, "Escort," resonated reassuringly in his mind.

"They'll take you to where the . . . Founder is. I'm certain he'll be very happy to meet you."

The Investigator had thanked the Psychologist, who had thereupon exited, leaving him in the company of a green plant, a water fountain—dry—and a pile of magazines placed on a low table. The Waiting Room was violently lighted and windowless. Like the Psychologist's office as well as the corridors they'd passed through, it was white, entirely white, its walls and floor covered with the same smooth yet spongy material that absorbed shocks as well as sounds.

As he looked at the floor and the walls and the violent light, as he remembered the Psychologist's words and the way he'd looked at him and listened to him, the Investigator suddenly felt an insidious malaise, to which, at first, he paid no attention. It was like an idea scratching at a distant door in a dwelling that comprised dozens of rooms and dozens of doors. Or, to transcribe another image that occurred to the Investigator, it was as if a person in a room on the fourth floor of a building had the impression that someone had just pressed the doorbell button outside the main door, but so briefly, so fleetingly, that the person in the fourth-floor apartment doesn't know if he heard the sound or imagined it. In any case, however, his perception of things is modified by it, he's no longer the same as he was a few seconds before the real or hypothetical ringing of the doorbell, and the actions he undertakes in the future will be influenced, one way or another, by what he heard or thought he heard.

Decidedly, the Waiting Room contained too much whiteness. Much too much whiteness. A world of whiteness, in which shapes as well as objects—all of them white as well—had a tendency to disappear: for example, the chair he was sitting on, the low table with the stack of magazines, the water fountain, and the pot that held the green plant, which had nothing green about it except its name (being itself totally white, with white leaves and white stems) and looked something like a large, bleached fern. After all, the Investigator thought, lingering for a moment over the plant's strange aspect, albino rabbits exist, why not albino ferns? And the whiteness all around him, in even the smallest details and smallest objects in that room, transported him, as pure, solidified snow produces an impression of serene, rigorous, simple beauty endowed with the power to rest both eye and mind.

The Investigator closed his eyes and passed from white to black. He stayed like that, with his eyelids shut, for a long time, trying to cut himself off from the whiteness surrounding him; for he had the feeling that it might absorb him, dissolve him, make him disappear, if he let himself go. He made an effort not to think about it too much. Not to let himself go, that was it. Be the Investigator. Don't forget to be the Investigator. Remain the Investigator. Keep being him, come what may.

He would no longer be surprised or dismayed by situations like the ones he'd been landing in for the past few days. After all, life is made up of impossible moments that come with no justification, are hard to interpret, and may not make any real sense. Life is nothing but a biological chaos one tries to organize and justify. But when the organization breaks down for some reason, whether because it's eroded away, inappropriate, obsolete, or because the person in charge of it has resigned, one finds himself facing up to events, emotions, questions, impasses, and illuminations piled on top of one another like blocks of ice, all of different sizes, carried along by heavy avalanches, and deposited in the shape of a pyramid with broken sides, balancing in unstable equilibrium on the edge of a great precipice.

The Investigator opened his eyes again and concentrated on what he was holding with both hands: the envelope bearing the words TO THE FOUNDER. Now, here was something tangible and indubitable. The Investigator felt the force of the object, of the actual, palpable object, whose material was in contact with the cells of his skin and the nerve endings implanted there, which in a millionth of a second transmitted to his consciousness the proof of the object's reality. This was nothing like some hypothetical doorbell that may have been rung or not! But why was he suddenly thinking about a doorbell?

He chased that thought away and picked up one of the magazines. There was neither a name nor a photograph on its glossy paper cover, which was blank and virgin white. He opened the magazine and flipped through it, increasingly nervous. Nothing. Every page was as milky-white as the cover. He took up a second magazine, then a third and a fourth, and finally went through them all. None of them contained a single printed character, the smallest illustration or photograph, or the tiniest drawing! They were all different from one another in format, thickness, or paper quality, but they were also all identical, because they all contained nothing! They were only gatherings of pages, pages whose whiteness was constant, uniform, monotonous. But the thing that most disturbed the Investigator, the thing that made him shivery and anxious, was that dozens, hundreds of fingers had leafed through those magazines, as demonstrated by the lower corners of the pages, which were dog-eared, crumpled, and sufficiently soiled to have gained an ivory patina. Those pages had been turned, or they'd been read. . . . If his eyes couldn't make anything out, did that mean no one else's could, either? Might he not be the victim of partial or selective blindness? Was it likely that anyone was printing, distributing, creating, or even imagining totally blank magazines? Magazines with no content? None whatsoever? And that people, whether idle, conditioned, or stupid, would read them all the same, spending their time and wearing out their eyes on pages empty of all information, of any text, of all photographs? What was to be gained from that? Yes, what could be the reason why individuals would devote time to reading what didn't exist?

The Investigator again felt feverish, nervous, uneasy. He threw the last magazine on the floor and pulled the Psychologist's envelope out from under his thigh.

TO THE FOUNDER. He reread the address three times. If he was reading it, that meant he had the ability to read it, and that it could be read. It followed, therefore, that those three words existed, written on the envelope. And it further followed that he was indeed able to read them and had not all at once—because of the shock of his collision with the wall, or because he'd abused his medications—become incapable of perceiving handwritten or printed characters. Wishing to be delivered from his doubts, without stopping to think, he ripped open the envelope and took out the sheet of paper the Psychologist had written on.

The paper was creamy white and folded in quarters, quite

carefully; the Investigator could still see the traces of the Psychologist's fingernails where he'd conscientiously pressed the edges of the folds. The Investigator unfolded the sheet of paper, looked at it, turned it over, turned it over again, and then started flipping it back and forth more and more violently, with trembling fingers. The sheet of paper was blank, dramatically blank, irremediably blank.

It bore no trace of ink, not a single word.

Nothing.

It was immaculate.

XXXVIII

MANY WARS AND MANY OTHER, less extreme circumstances have tested man's faculty of resistance, subjecting him to physical and mental trials whose ongoing refinement, from century to century, serves to demonstrate the human being's capacity for surpassing himself in the imagination and execution of horror.

From simple drops of water falling one after another on a prisoner's forehead to the Pear of Anguish, from torture with the boot, on the wheel, by drawing and quartering, by the inoculation of gangrene into healthy bodies, by the insertion of living rats into the vagina of a female victim, by the peremptory amputation of all four limbs, by the sun, to which one leaves the task of baking the skull of a naked creature buried up to the neck in desert sand, by slowly removing a hundred strips of flesh from a living body with a knife, by plunging a child into a tub of icy water so that the duration of its death agony may be accurately timed, by shocks of electricity, by inflicting upon a man the spectacle of his wife, his daughter, his son executed with a bullet in the back of the head, by the traditional and constant use of rape, by disemboweling, by prolonged detention in precarious conditions, by forced nudity intended as humiliation, by the blade, deliberately chosen for rust and dullness, that gradually slices through a victim's throat, and by endless solitude, to the conviction planted in the victim's mind that he himself is solely responsible for the situation he's in and for the tortures being inflicted upon him, man has revealed himself to be not a wolf to man, despite the ancient saying—an old saw unfair to wolves, which are genuinely civilized and socialized creatures—but, more accurately, the anti-man, as physicists speak of antimatter.

Who wanted to destroy the Investigator, then? Who was it who was so determined to grind him down like a common grain of wheat and scatter the poor flour to the wind, never to return? Who, and why? For this was the conclusion he'd come to in the soundless privacy of the white room, a conclusion in the form of a double question. Well beyond his hunger and his thirst, well beyond time, whose passage he couldn't—or could no longer—quantify, having had his nose rubbed in its irrefutable relativity, well beyond pure questions of identity—who was he, really?—the Investigator was gradually apprehending the void in which he floated and out of which he was made. Had he not himself become a portion of matter confronted with antimatter in expansion? Was he not progressing, swiftly or slowly, it made little difference, toward the black hole that was going to ingest him? Did someone—but who? who?—want to bring him face-to-face with a radical, definitive, metaphorical insight into his life, into human life in general?

The Investigator doubted his thoughts as well as his faculty of thinking. In the absence of any reference point—how could one cling to whiteness, to magazines composed of vanished texts, to a green plant that wasn't even green?—he persuaded himself that perhaps he wasn't completely living, and therefore not completely thinking. I don't think, he thought. Someone's thinking through me, or, rather, someone's thinking me. No initiative is within my possibilities. I'm made to believe that I have an Investigation to conduct. In reality, doubtless, I have no such thing. I'm tossed back and forth, bashed around, bruised and then petted, knocked over and then stood upright again. I'm placed and displaced. I'm forbidden to cross a street and then I'm led across it. I'm smiled upon, I'm embraced, I'm cheered, only to be dashed the next minute against a wall. My brain is washed with floods of rain and avalanches of snow, with waves of cold and heat, I'm starved, I'm dehydrated, I'm stuffed with food, I'm made to vomit, I'm humiliated by the ridiculous clothes I'm compelled to wear, I'm prevented from washing myself, I'm walled up in a room, I'm listened to patiently in order to be all the more quickly abandoned to my fate. What justification can I seek for all that?

The Investigator would have paid dearly to be able to go backward, to be a reel of film that could be rewound, to make a long march in reverse, gradually returning to the train and its steps, thin rectangles of open-worked metal he should never have gone down, to the train compartment, which he scarcely remembered, then to his apartment on the morning of his departure—but he was too tired to visualize his apartment, and he would have been incapable of describing it or even of giving its exact address, to say nothing of the furnishings or the floor covering (carpet? tiles? parquet?) or the walls (painted? wallpapered?)—and then, finally, back to the Head of Section's office at the moment when he'd spoken to him of his mission. The Investigator wondered what exact terms had been employed; they were difficult to recall.

At that very moment, which could still have been dated, even if dating it was no longer of any use, he had another thought without any logical basis, a dazzling illumination destined to die at once, like big fireworks in the dark skies of summer nights: He felt that all the places he'd passed through, all the streets he'd gone down, the walls he'd walked past, the buildings he'd seen, the first night's bar, the Hotel and the Guardhouse, the glass cone where the Manager's office was, and maybe even the Psychologist's office, no longer existed—from a certain point of view, he was right—and that in fact they had existed only for the brief moment of his passage, and that no doubt the same went for the people he'd encountered, who had likewise disappeared, annihilated along with their settings, plunged into the endless torpor for which the Guide's Level 6 Impediment was a metaphor, and that this universal, complete, irreversible disappearance perhaps signaled the failure of his memory and the exhaustion of his intellectual and physical faculties, which no longer allowed him to retain anything, and that he was now getting ready to become a person who, quite simply, would soon cease to be a person at all, would meet the fate of all other people, who wind up dying one day even if, throughout the course of their existence, they have never stopped denying the implacable evidence.

At the same time, the thought of the destruction of his thoughts, the awareness that the whiteness that surrounded him and had contaminated everything in sight, both walls and furniture, surely prefigured the greater, limitless white-

ness toward which he was moving—this very thought proved
that he was, in spite of everything, still thinking! And that
the hope of remaining, of lasting a while longer, even if
it was only a very little while, existed. All his misadven-
tures, his crash into the wall, his obsession with seeing the
Founder's portrait everywhere, and his isolation in whiteness
had as yet failed to destroy him completely. The Investigator
turned out to be quite solid, unshaken even in his awareness
of impending disappearance. But how sorrowful all that was!
He couldn't take it anymore, the mad race going on inside the
walls of his skull. And he was starting to get cold. Very cold.

He grabbed the bottom of his light, too light, hospital
gown and tried in vain to stretch it, to lengthen it, to pull it
over a little more of his body; but by twisting the fabric he
succeeded only in tearing it at the left shoulder, and it was at
that moment, at the precise moment when he was performing the very human action of clothing himself, of covering
his naked skin with an article of clothing, that the walls and
floor of the Waiting Room started moving, as if the movement had been synchronized with the ripping of the gown,
which made a delicate sound like opening a zipper, and a few
fractions of a second later, in proportion as the trembling of
the floor and the walls increased, a metallic racket broke out
and gathered force, a concerted din of axles set in motion,
wheels, squeals, clangs, and bangs that caused an image to
spring up in the Investigator's brain, a very distinct image of
the train that had brought him to the City and whose dilapi-
dated condition had surprised him a little, even though he
hadn't really dwelled on it, yes, that train sprang up in his
memory, along with many others, dozens, hundreds, thousands of trains, their engines united and their cars filled with

resigned travelers, all of whom had features more or less in common with those of the Investigator, all of them tossed about, powerless, surprised, and together making up, in spite of themselves, the interminable and stupefied procession of human History.

The pitching increased, and so did the racket. While both grew in magnitude, the sounds of whistles, of hammer blows, and perhaps of voices, too, though he wasn't sure about that, seemed to transpire through the padded surfaces around him, literally to transpire, the clamor changing into drops of sweat, of oily, sticky liquid, a kind of resin seeping in from outside and suffusing the white walls, penetrating them, passing through them, and saturating the room.

The Investigator would have liked to puncture his ears so he wouldn't hear anymore, pierce his eyes so he wouldn't see anymore, burst his soul so he'd stop suffering this nightmare, but he couldn't do any of that. The room was flinging him in every direction, contradictory forces were crushing him, spinning him, sending him flying to the ceiling, the ceiling that changed into the floor, then into a side wall, and then again into the ceiling, just before it violently became the floor again. Despite all this nonstop banging around, the Investigator felt no physical pain. Everything was soft. The shocks were cushioned, and whenever an object—low table, chair, magazine, green plant that was white—struck him, he had no sensation at all, just the impression that the object was going through him without causing any pain or damage. He thought about the men whom the Species, for the past several decades, had regularly been sending into space in order to explore its confines or ridiculously, and quite briefly, to take possession of it. He remembered seeing some of those men floating in the air of their cabin, pirouetting, sucking up liquids that remained in suspension in the form of little drops of different sizes and various colors, playing with wrenches that had assumed the weight of feathers and steel balls no heavier than soap bubbles. He remembered their slow voices, muddled and staticky from the hundreds of thousands of miles they'd had to travel to reach Earth, and the slow-motion smile on their faces, and how they were shut up in a narrow space, far from the world, zipping through the universe at astronomical speeds, alone, with no real possibility of return nor desire to return. Yes, he remembered their smile, an eternal smile that no longer had anything terrestrial or human about it, loosed as they were from the original blue globe, which took on for them the proportions of a child's ball, small and far away.

Then he too began to smile, and he let himself go.

XXXIX

A RAY OF WHITE INCANDESCENT LIGHT had been striking the Investigator's left eyelid for the past several
minutes. Eventually, feeling the heat, he opened the
eye but closed it at once; the light was impossibly dazzling.
He tried to open his other eye, but with no more success. The
light was simply too fierce. He shifted his head and body a
little and half opened his eyelids again. Sparing his eyes,
the light now fell hard on his neck. The lock on the door had
given way, and the light was streaming in through the narrow opening.

The Investigator came completely awake and looked
around him. The Waiting Room had been turned upside
down, the chairs and table were broken, the livid plant lay
sprawled in the ruins of its pot. The magazines looked like
shavings from enormous, chlorotic tubers. He stood up and
touched his body, expecting it to fall into a thousand pieces,
but he was all right. The rip in his gown, however, was worse
than before and now left two-thirds of his torso uncovered.

A little fearful, he pushed open the door, slowly, and then,
since nothing frightening happened, he flung it open with
some force, so that it thudded against the outside wall. The
sun rushed in like water through a suddenly lifted sluice

gate. The light, he realized, was coming from the sun, only the sun, which beat down on him ferociously. It was a pale-yellow ball of fire, a circle with a shimmering circumference suspended above the horizon. He couldn't tell whether the ball was moving away from the horizon or preparing to dissolve in it. The Investigator made a visor of his hands. Thus protected, he was gradually able to take stock of the place where he found himself.

It was a sort of immense vacant lot, dusty and perfectly flat. Scattered here and there, according to some incomprehensible arrangement, were stacks of containers. They resembled big trailers without wheels, some of them sheathed in steel or aluminum, armored parallelepipeds incandescently reflecting the sunlight, whereas others were wrecked and looked like giant, battered cardboard cartons. There were also many site sheds, with plasterboard or pressed wood or sheet-metal walls. Sometimes a group of them were in perfect alignment; others were shoved together in clumps, lopsided, tipped up, overturned, resting on their sides. A few containers stood in isolation; although there was no sign on the ground of a border or an enclosure or a boundary, a prudent distance was apparently maintained around them. In certain groups, hierarchies of size, shape, material, or condition, whether good or bad, seemed to hold sway. Some containers were brand-new, as if they'd just come off an assembly line; others, by contrast, showed evidence of decay in the corrosion of their component parts, the dirty stains covering their original surfaces, the fanciful geometry of their wall assemblies.

The Investigator moved forward a few paces. The heat was stifling, and the sun didn't move. There was no indication that it was going to set, just as there was none that it would rise higher. The day was suspended, scorching; it had neither evening nor morning and was distinguished not by its place in a classic temporal sequence but by the immobility of its light and its heat. The whiteness of the ground, which was covered with soil that resembled plaster, prevented the Investigator from really being able to take in his surroundings. He could make out things in the foreground fairly clearly, could discern the dozens and dozens of containers located not far from him, but beyond that, and despite all his efforts, he couldn't see at all, because everything disappeared in the wobbly fluctuations of the air, which dilated the atmosphere into moving, translucent fumaroles, and behind them the landscape collapsed in an unfathomable void.

The Enterprise couldn't be far off, or the City, either. His journey in the container hadn't lasted very long, or at least that was his impression. But, then again, what did he know?

He was almost naked, and even though he'd left the Waiting Room only a short time before, twenty seconds at the most, his head and body were covered with sweat. (No doubt to convince himself that everything was going to return to normal, he continued to think of the burst prefabricated structure lying ten feet away from him with its door open as the Waiting Room.) He felt extremely light. Walking—he took a few steps—was easy. The only problem was the heat. He'd never known such heat. It was thoroughly upsetting, because, aside from cooking him, it extracted from his body a great deal of perspiration, which slicked his legs, dripped between his thighs, ran down his back, his chest, the nape of his neck, his sides, his forehead, flowed uninterruptedly and especially into his eyes, drowning them, adding liquid blinding to light blinding, with the result that the Investigator not only couldn't see much, he was also steadily seeing less and less.

With his arms and hands stretched out toward emptiness, hoping in vain to block a sun that was slipping in everywhere, as if his limbs had become transparent, the Investigator looked for shade. He walked in all directions, and in particular he circled the Waiting Room, but it did no good, he couldn't find the least shadow, which defied all logic and all laws of physics, for if the sun was shining on one wall, it couldn't be shining on the opposite wall, too, and, what was more, the great star was far from its zenith, contenting itself with hovering lethargically just over the horizon; but the Investigator had reached the point where nothing surprised him anymore.

Out of breath, he stopped, sat—or, rather, knelt—on the ground, folded his body at the waist, drew his chin down to his breastbone, curled his head under himself as far as he could, and put one hand on each temple, getting smaller and smaller, a shape deposited on the ground, nothing but a shape, hardly different from a large stone or a package; had there been anyone to see it, he might have wondered what it could possibly contain. And what *did* he contain, in fact, aside from several score pounds of burning, ill-used flesh, inhabited by a buffeted, uncertain, and broken soul?

The Investigator had no more tears. Even if he'd wanted to cry, he wouldn't have been able to. All the water in him was leaving his body in the form of sweat. He groaned and groaned again, trying to get more of his head between his arms and under his torso in order to escape the sun. His groaning became a cry. At first it was low and comparatively muffled, but then it grew, throbbed, rumbled, conveying the last shudders of an energy that sensed its own imminent decline, and culminating in a final explosion of animal howling, extended and powerful, which might have caused chills in a hearer had it not been so hot.

In zoos, it sometimes happens that the cries of the great apes or the peacocks awaken the other animals, and then, in the middle of the night or during the peaceful afternoon hours, when everything's asleep and there's no hint of unrest, a sonorous protest breaks out, a sort of living tempest consisting of hundreds of sounds and voices fused together into a thunder of low notes and high notes, of whistling spasms and guttural bursts, of yelping, hooting, growling, stamping, of banged bars and shaken wire fences, of barking and trumpeting, which electrifies the passerby and plunges him into a nightmare all the more frightening because he's unable to discern the exact source of each of the sounds that scamper around him, bind him tightly, and suffocate him, preventing his escape from the cacophony as it turns into torture.

The Investigator hadn't completely finished howling when, from most of the containers, gigantic boxes, prefabricated buildings, mobile homes, and storage units scattered around him, there arose a clamor, partly muffled and partly clear, of cries, rattles, rumblings, of voices, yes, no doubt about it, voices, whose supplicant tones he could grasp without understanding the words, the voices of ghosts or of persons condemned to death, the voices of the dying, of outcasts, age-old, ancestral, and at the same time atrociously present, voices that surrounded the Investigator and drowned out his own.

XL

FTER A WHILE, THE VOICES fell silent. Gradually. One by one. It was a progressive disappearance, as if a knowing finger, in the name of a higher intention, had turned down a dial that regulated their intensity. The Investigator couldn't get over it. He spun around and around, making himself dizzy, and finally came to a staggering halt.

"Is anyone there?" he ventured to ask after a few seconds.

"Here!"

"Over here!"

"Me!"

"Please!"

"I'm here!"

"Me! Me!"

At different volumes, depending on their distance but also on the reserves of energy quickening them, the voices made themselves heard again, at first isolated but then mingled, confused, blending into one another, creating an intolerable commotion that seemed to saturate the air, filling it like fog or heavy rain.

The Investigator ran over to the nearest container and knocked on its wall. At once, blows struck from the inside responded to him.

"Who are you?" the Investigator asked, pressing one ear against the wall.

"Open the door, for pity's sake, let me out. . . . I can't take anymore . . ." replied the muffled voice from inside the container.

"But who are you?" the Investigator repeated.

"I'm . . . I'm . . ."

The voice hesitated and broke off. The Investigator thought he could hear sobbing. "Tell me who you are!" he said.

"I was . . . I was . . . the Investigator."

The Investigator jumped back as if he'd just burned himself. His heart was racing.

"Don't go away, please, don't leave me . . . please. . . ."

The Investigator's chest contracted under violent pressure. The beating of his heart was uncontrollable and totally random, now slowing down, now most unexpectedly accelerating. He placed a hand over it, trying to calm and reassure it, as though it were an animal with one leg caught in a snare and striving to free itself, against all logic, by gnawing off the leg rather than biting through the cord. The pause did him good. With the back of his hand, he wiped away the sweat that continued to stream down his forehead, giving him the impression that he was dissolving.

He examined the container. It was one of those that appeared to be the most recent, the newest. The film of dust that covered it was thin and translucent. Careful to make as little noise as possible, he started walking around the container, looking for the door.

"I can hear you, you know. You're moving. . . ."

The Investigator kept walking. He made an effort not to

worry about the voice, which had spoken those last words in the most desperate manner possible. He stepped along on tiptoe, making himself light. Rounding one corner of the container, he looked at the wall on that end, saw no door, and tiptoed on.

"Why don't you answer me . . . ?"

The Investigator continued his inspection. He turned the next corner and studied the second of the container's two long sides. Still nothing. No door in sight.

". . . just say a word, please, I know you're still there. . . . I know it. . . ."

There was but one side left. Only one. The Investigator increased his pace. The man in the container could hear him, so there was no longer any point in walking so cautiously. Anyway, why should he be scared? The man didn't seem to be aggressive, and besides, he was shut up inside a box. The Investigator was about to turn the last corner, but he slowed down. Or, rather, his body slowed down, even before his mind gave the order. Why was he so fearful? What exactly was he afraid of? What discovery was he anticipating, and why did the thought of it paralyze him to such a degree? He knew the answer but dared not admit it to himself. He'd inspected three of the container's four sides, and there was no door, no opening at all, in any of the walls. That meant, therefore, that the door was located on the fourth side. To make sure of that, all he had to do was to go around the final corner and take a look. However, he didn't do it. He dared not do it. He dared not because, deep down inside, he was convinced there was no door and no window on the fourth side, either, even though that didn't make any sense.

The Investigator let himself slide down to the ground

and sat with his back against the container. He preferred not to verify. He preferred to cling to doubt. Only doubt, he told himself, would allow him to hold on a little while longer. For there were only two possibilities: Either there was a door on the fourth side of the container, or there was not. If his eyes saw the door, then all would be well. But if his eyes verified the absence of a door, then there would be nothing left for him but to sink all the way into madness or just let himself get baked by that bloody sun, which was still there, still in the same place, sending its heat streaming out over the naked land. The Investigator preferred not to know about the door and clung to the possibility, the meager possibility, that he was still in a world where enclosed structures couldn't contain anything, no object, no person, no plant, discolored or not, unless there was an opening in the structure through which the contents had passed.

"You're still there, aren't you?"

The container's voice was very close. It echoed in the Investigator's back—the man must have spoken with his mouth against the wall. His words entered the Investigator's body, causing a kind of tickling.

"Answer me. . . ."

"Who are you?" the Investigator asked again.

"I already told you, I'm the Investigator."

"But *I'm* the Investigator!"

There was a silence, and then he thought he heard a sigh.

"If you say so . . . In any case, we all are, more or less . . ."

"I don't understand."

"Think what you wish. I'm not going to fight, I don't have any more strength. . . . It's ruined me, all this. Please, can you help me get out of here?"

"I'm afraid not. Your box looks like it's hermetically sealed."

"Box? But I was asked to take a seat in the Waiting Room. . . ."

The Investigator moved a little away from the wall of the container and looked at it again. Then he said, "I said 'box' for brevity's sake. In fact, you're imprisoned in a sort of prefabricated building located in the middle of nowhere."

"Nowhere . . ."

The voice fell silent. The Investigator didn't know what to do. He felt that there was, on the other side of the wall, a man who—except perhaps for a few differences—had experienced events similar to those he himself had been confronted with.

"It's cold, it's so cold . . ." the voice murmured.

"How can you say that?" the Investigator asked in surprise. His body was visibly liquefying, dissolving in fluids, in water, in sweat. "I have practically no clothes on, and I'm still too hot. The sun looks like it's suspended in the sky. It doesn't move an inch. There's not a scrap of cloud, and when a little wind comes up, all it does is blow streams of burning dust into the heat!"

"How lucky for you . . . No matter how I wrap myself up in my clothes, I'm still chilled to the bone. There are ice crystals everywhere, in my beard, on my hands, on the wall, on the low table, and even on the green plant, which is all white anyway. I can't feel my hands or my feet anymore, they seem to be frozen, I think they're already dead. . . ."

The container didn't appear to be a walk-in cooler, and its outer walls, plywood covered with a coat of beige paint, felt hot to the touch. Couldn't the voice be lying to him? Wasn't this just another of the numerous tests he'd had to undergo?

"What was the subject of your Investigation?" the Investigator asked.

"I was supposed . . . I was supposed to . . . Oh, what's the use of explaining. . . ."

The voice had lost all its strength. The Investigator had to press his ear against the container wall as hard as he could in order to make out the words.

"Were you investigating the Suicides within the Enterprise?" the Investigator persisted.

"The Enterprise? Suicides? No . . . no . . . My job was to . . . I mean, I was supposed to try to . . . explain . . . the decrease of motivation within the Group. . . . So cold . . . cold . . . My lips are freezing, too, and my eyes, I can't see anymore. . . ."

"Which Group? What are you talking about?"

"The Group . . . the Group . . ."

"Does the Group belong to the Enterprise?"

"The Enterprise . . . ?"

"Make an effort, damn it!" cried the Investigator, losing patience. "If you're where you are, there's bound to be a reason, for God's sake! One doesn't wind up where you are without a good reason! The Group you're talking about must be part of the Enterprise. Answer me!"

"Group . . . motivation . . . tongue . . . frozen . . . Enterprise . . . can't anymore . . . can't anymore . . ."

"Answer me!!!"

". . . anymore . . ."

The Investigator began to shout, beating the walls of the box with both hands, abandoning the relatively hushed tones he'd been using up to that point. And thereupon, dozens, hundreds, thousands (or were there more? who could know?) of walled-up voices were raised once again, in an outburst of cries, yells, death rattles, tragic appeals, complaints, prayers, and supplications that made the Investigator feel as though he were being clawed at from every side, clung to like some wretched boat that shipwreck victims cling to, even though they know it won't be able to save them all, continuing to hold on to it all the same, with the sole, selfish intention of sinking it so that it won't save anyone, unconsciously preferring the deaths of all to the survival of even one.

The Investigator could find but one escape from all that: He clapped his hands over his ears and closed his eyes.

XLI

Q UITE OFTEN, WE TRY TO GRASP what escapes our
understanding by using terms and concepts peculiar to
ourselves. Ever since man attained distinction among
the other species, he hasn't stopped measuring the universe
and the laws governing it by the scale of his thought and its
products, without always noticing the inadequacy of such an
approach. Nonetheless, he knows very well, for example, that
a sieve is not a proper tool for carrying water. Why, then, does
he constantly fool himself into thinking his mind can grasp
everything and comprehend everything? Why not, rather,
recognize that his mind is an ordinary, everyday sieve, a tool
that renders undeniable service in certain circumstances,
performing specific actions in given situations, but is completely useless in many others, because it's not made for them,
because it's got holes in it, because a great many things pass
through it before it can hold them back and consider them,
even if only for a few seconds?

Was it because of the unrelenting heat? Was it because he
couldn't stop sweating, seeping, disappearing into his fluids?
Was it because he was thirsty without even being completely
aware of it that the Investigator was starting to think about
human imperfection, about liquids and a sieve?

All was silent again. He still had his eyes closed. He'd dropped his hands long ago, and now they lay along his sides. The voices had stopped. Only the moaning of the wind as it played among the containers reached his ears. All of a sudden, he had the impression that he was a little less hot, and at the same time, the blackness behind his eyelids became still blacker.

A shadow.

It must be a shadow, he thought, a thick cloud hiding the sun, unless the sun itself has finally decided to go down.

He opened his eyes. A man stood before him, a figure he could see only in silhouette. The tall, stout body cast a large shadow over the Investigator. The man looked enormous. He was no cloud. In his right hand, he was holding what appeared to be a broom handle.

"Where did you come from?" asked the Shadow. His was an old man's voice, heavy, deep, a little hoarse, but it projected, despite that roughness, a lively, fresh, lightly ironic tone. The other voices, the ones that came from inside the containers, rose in lamentation again.

"*Be quiet!*" the Shadow bellowed, and immediately there was silence. The Investigator couldn't believe it. Who could this shadow be, that he had such rough, incontestable authority over all those captives?

"I asked you a question," the Shadow said, addressing the Investigator again.

"The Waiting Room. I was in the Waiting Room, over there . . ." the Investigator slowly replied, leaning on the wall of the container as he rose, with great difficulty, to his feet. The Shadow moved, turning his head in the direction

the Investigator had indicated, and then remained still for
a few moments, gazing at the gutted prefab structure with
the open door from which the Investigator had emerged. The
latter had the sun in his eyes again, the bloody, blinding sun.
It hadn't moved an inch.

"You can't see a thing," said the Shadow. "Wait, I'll fix
that for you."

The Investigator felt a hand on his person, tearing away
what was left of his hospital gown. He quickly tried to cover
his groin, but the cavernous voice forestalled him: "You're not
going to start with that old nonsense again, are you? What's
the point? Nobody can see you, except for me, and I'm in the
same state as you."

The Investigator heard the Shadow tearing his hospital
gown into many strips. Then his hands, his old hands with
their long, misshapen fingers, grazed the Investigator's face
as they tied the strips around his eyes in several layers, gently
pulling the cloth taut and knotting each strip behind his
head, but not too tightly, so that his eyelids would retain their
freedom of movement.

"There you are. It's done. You can open your eyes now."

When he did so, the Investigator perceived the world
through the orangey gauze that up until then had served him
as a garment. The sun was now only a yellow ball the color
of straw, and the ground had lost its blinding whiteness. Here
and there, he could make out darker masses: the unequal
hulks of the different containers. They covered the plain,
which was perfectly flat, without elevation or eminence, as
far as the eye could see. There weren't dozens or hundreds
of them, as he'd at first thought, but thousands, dozens of

thousands! And the vision of that infinity sent sweetish bile surging up into his dry mouth. He felt on the point of vomiting. But what could he possibly have to vomit?

In each of those boxes, he told himself, there was a man, a man like him, a man who'd been knocked about, mistreated, allowed to hope, who'd been made to believe that he had a mission to accomplish, a role to play, a place in life, who'd been driven crazy, humiliated, brought low, who'd seen the fragility of his condition, his memory, and his certainties repeatedly demonstrated, an Investigator, perhaps, or someone claiming to be an Investigator, a man who was now howling and pounding the walls, and whom nobody could ever help. A man who could have been him if his box, less solid or more abused than the others, hadn't opened.

For such a long time, he'd thought himself unique; now he was able to measure the magnitude of his error, and it terrified him.

"That's better, isn't it?"

The Investigator started. He'd almost forgotten the Shadow.

"Here, it's by blindfolding yourself that you're able to see."

The Shadow was becoming more distinct, as a mirage sometimes does. The Investigator could make out his features and the details of his body. He was decidedly an old man, with a distended paunch that fell in several folds and hid his sex. The skin of his thighs put the Investigator in mind of very ancient animals, members of species that vanished ages ago, and his sunken pectoral muscles resembled the withered breasts of an elderly wet-nurse. His shoulders sagged, too, presenting soft, round, receding contours attached to obese arms on which the skin hung like tattered spiderwebs. But when the Investigator raised his eyes to the Shadow's face, his shock was so great that he felt the earth vanishing under his feet and would have fallen had the other not held him up with his right hand, while his left retained its grasp on the broom handle, which apparently served him as both cane and scepter. The broad forehead, on which a network of wrinkles etched deltas and streamlets; the drooping jowls; the dimpled chin; the ears, behind which his silvery hair cascaded in gray waves; the heavy mustache, whose thick points descended on either side of his mouth, with its cracked lips—those were features the Investigator had contemplated many times, and even though he couldn't make out the eyes, which disappeared almost completely behind the blindfold, he nevertheless had to acknowledge the overwhelming evidence: "The Founder!" he managed to blurt out, feeling waves of electricity surging through his body. "You're the Founder!"

"The Founder?" the Shadow repeated. He seemed to reflect for a while, and then he shrugged. "If it makes you happy . . . I'm not in the habit of being contrary. On the other hand, if there's one thing I'm certain of, it's that you're the first man."

"The First Man . . . ?"

"Yes, the first to come out of one of those boxes. No one was ever so lucky before. But don't kid yourself, you're only getting a brief reprieve. You'll wind up like the others. Whether you're inside or outside doesn't change anything. That's the distinctive characteristic of this ship; everyone's aboard, one way or another."

The Shadow dealt the container a heavy blow, which provoked no reaction on the inside. "You see? It's all over for him. He must have breathed his last. These boxes are so well designed and so well sealed that any attempt to open them is useless. I often tried my hand on one or another of them, for philanthropic reasons, no doubt, or to relieve my boredom. I gave up after breaking three fingernails and spraining my wrist."

Joining the deed to the word, the Shadow massaged his forearm, as if his evocation of the incident had reawakened the pain. "What's curious," he went on, "is to discover that the weight of misfortune becomes fairly light in proportion as it intensifies or proliferates. Seeing a man die before your eyes is quite unpleasant. Almost unbearable. To see or hear millions die dilutes both atrociousness and compassion. Rather quickly, you find you no longer feel very much about what happened. Number is the enemy of emotion. Who has ever felt bad while trampling an anthill, can you tell me that? Nobody, that's who. I talk to them sometimes, to keep them company when I've got nothing better to do, but they're tiresome. . . . They want me to put myself in their place, but it never occurs to a single one of them to put himself in mine. I'd like to make them feel better, but all they know how to do is complain. Some of them still have telephones. They try to reach their loved ones or some emergency-services number, but they exhaust their credit or their battery in the mazes of the automatic switchboards, which never manage to put them in touch with the person they want to reach. Besides, even if they made contact, what could the person on the other end do for them? What could we do? Nothing, as I already told you. After all, I'm not responsible for putting them where they are. And if I did have some responsibility at some point, it was so long ago that the statute of limitations has run out by now."

There was a silence. It lasted a fraction of a second or a thousand years, how could he know? Time had become an accessory dimension. The Investigator's body was visibly melting. He was departing bit by bit, baked by the sun, squeezed and twisted like a rag that's wrung out one last time before being thrown into the garbage.

"Quite fortunately," the Shadow resumed, "these poor creatures never last very long. In the beginning, they howl like pigs getting their throats slit, but they start to weaken very soon, and in the end they quiet down. Forever. The big silence. Why would anyone hold that against *me*? What a funny idea! What can I do? As if I had anything to do with it! To each his destiny. Do you think it's easy to sweep up here? One gets what one deserves. There are no innocents. Don't you believe that?"

"I don't know. . . . I don't know anymore . . ." the Investigator declared. "Where are we? In Hell?"

The Shadow nearly choked and then burst out laughing, a huge laugh that ended in a horrible coughing fit. He cleared his throat and spat three times, very far.

"In Hell! The things you say! You like simplistic explanations, don't you? These days I don't think that works anymore. The world is too complex. The old tricks are worn out. And besides, people are no longer children who can still be told tall tales. No, you're simply here in a sort of transit zone of the Enterprise. Over time, this area has been transformed into a big, open-air dumping ground. Whatever's out of service, whatever can't be put elsewhere is piled up here: things, objects, junk no one knows what to do with. I could show you entire hills composed of prostheses, wooden legs, soiled bandages, pharmaceutical waste, valleys filled with the cadavers of mobile phones, computers, printed circuit boards, silicon, lakes loaded to the brim with Freon, toxic sludge, acids, geological faults plugged with great shovelfuls of radioactive material and bituminous sands, to say nothing of rivers carrying along millions of gallons of waste oil, chemical fertilizers, solvents, pesticides, forests whose trees are bundles of rusty scrap iron, metallic structures embellished with reinforced concrete, melted plastic amalgamated with millions of tons of used syringes, which end up looking like defoliated branches, and I forget the rest. What do you want me to do? I can't clean up everything for them—this is all I've got!"

The Shadow punctuated his words by waving his broom.

"There's nothing here yet," he went on. "It's new territory. A landscape in progress, waiting for the artists who'll celebrate it at some future date and the families that will come here, sooner or later, for Sunday outings and picnics. We're just at the beginning. Only containers are arriving at the moment, prefabricated structures built in haste according to need. The Enterprise is expanding so fast. One may well wonder who the head of it is, because, try as I may, I can't understand his strategy. The Enterprise needs new business locations, but it gets rid of them just as quickly as it acquires them, because at the same time it's constantly being restructured, and sometimes regrettable errors occur, mistakes that inevitably entail a certain number of victims. The production rates imposed are such that the Transporters load the containers even as people are still working on them. Bad luck for the workers, but they just have to make sure they get out in time. Distraction comes at a high price these days, and so does excessive zeal. Overtime hours dig the graves of those who accumulate them. The age of the utopians is over.

Later, people will still be able to buy pipe dreams, on credit, from antique shops or collectors or village flea markets, but for what purpose? To show them to the children? Will there still be children? Do you have children? Have you reproduced yourself? In our time, man is a negligible quantity, a secondary species with a talent for disaster. He's no longer anything at this point but a risk that has to be run."

The Shadow spat again, ejecting a fat, slimy, greenish gob that landed in the dust, forming there a narrow-bodied, oblong-headed snake that sank into the ground without further ado.

"So, according to you," the Shadow went on, looking at the Investigator through his blindfold, "what am I supposed to have founded?"

XLII

THE INVESTIGATOR FELT DISTINCTLY that he was on the point of absenting himself for good. He wondered if perhaps he hadn't already done so. His existence was continuing only intermittently now, in the manner of a dotted line or a blinking neon tube that makes a sound like fragile insects when they fly too close to streetlights on summer evenings and get burned to cinders. He was reduced to living in fits and starts, in brief breaks of consciousness interspersed by black holes, deep tar-pits in which nothing happened, nothing he could remember.

And it was neither hunger nor thirst nor weariness that was the cause of his steep decline. It wasn't even the unbroken series of obstacles that had littered his path. At bottom, what undermined the final defenses of his soul—the part that was still protected behind the few remaining ramparts and still generating a little sense, whereas the walls, the watchtowers, the moats, the drawbridges, the sentry posts had all been destroyed in a progressive collapse, a sapping operation that had begun with his arrival in the City—was the disappointment of discovering that he'd been a workman in futility, that he would never have had sufficient strength to accomplish the mission assigned to him, namely to understand why men had chosen to kill themselves, why some had decided, at a certain point in their existence, to retire from the game of Humanity and not to wait for the ineluctable degeneration of the organism, the rupture of an aneurysm, the proliferation of metastasis, the obstruction of one of their principal arteries by fat accumulations, a vehicular or domestic accident, murder, drowning, an outbreak of germ warfare, a bombing, an earthquake, a tsunami, or a major flood to end their lives. Why had a number of men—five, ten, twenty or so, thousands; exactly how many made little difference—acted against their most deeply rooted instinct, which commanded them to survive at all costs, to continue the struggle, to accept the unacceptable, because the religion of life must perforce be stronger than the despair caused by endless obstacles? Why had some men—whether within the Enterprise or elsewhere was of quite minor importance—thrown in the towel, handed over their badges, turned in their manly uniforms? How could he, a simple Investigator, a poor wretch, ever have understood and explained that?

Malfunction became the essence of the Investigator's being. Shaken by an ongoing, irreversible short-circuit, he struggled in a confusion of instants that his exhausted mind turned into a collage made up of moments he'd lived through, hallucinations, dreams, fantasies, memories, and anticipations; and the bombardment of images to which he was subjected and which he couldn't evade finished the breakup of his consciousness, fragmenting it as a grenade touches the ground and blasts its various shards into a rainbow of death.

"You haven't answered my question. Is this a common practice with you?" the Founder demanded.

"What question?" murmured the Investigator, who had

just re-entered, in a very temporary fashion, the last scene he'd been in, the one in which the unmoving sun flung down its heat ever more intolerably. "I've been toyed with, haven't I? I'm not up to it. I'm not up to my life. And that sun . . . Isn't it just a simple light shining through a big magnifying glass above my head? Am I still under observation? Tell me. Is the experiment still going on? Have I passed the previous tests? Please tell me: Am I going to be able to investigate?"

"You answer my question with questions. A rather facile strategy, don't you think?" The Shadow's voice sounded irritated. "We've been together now for I don't know how long, I have put up with you, and I'm waiting for your answer. What do you imagine? You think I know more about it than you do? Sometimes you tinker a bit, you invent, and everything blows up in your hands. You'd like to stop the ensuing catastrophe, but it's too late! So what can you do? Mope? No, not me. I simply decided to turn my back. Cowardice isn't the failing it's thought to be. Courage often causes more harm. Let them figure it out!"

The Investigator could no longer understand what the Shadow was saying to him. He didn't feel he was walking away; it seemed to him, rather, that his body was floating in the air and he wasn't really touching the ground. His arms had taken on the consistency of fog. Of his hands, as dense as a cloud of incense, only the palms remained, volatile and ashen; the light was already passing through them, revealing billions of particles agitated by contradictory currents, by majestic shocks that carried them off in waves, in whirlwinds, in spirals, hurling them into shafts where they became stars in the midst of darkness, forming innumerable Milky Ways, in the midst of which could be seen the mauve glow of explosions, the radiance of universal cataclysms, the sensational collisions of asteroids, comets, and other bodies launched at the dawn of time into the purest void.

"Don't worry about anything anymore," the Shadow went on. "Stop being concerned about yourself. Your fingers won't come back. Nor will the rest. It's all going to be eaten away, little by little, you can't do anything about it, and in any case it's painless. I guarantee you that. But try to answer my question—you still could if you wanted to. Take advantage of your extraordinarily lucky escape from the container, try to give it some meaning, and answer my question: What is it you think I've founded?"

The Shadow's voice coiled around the Investigator, penetrated him, slipped into what remained of his chest, filled his whole skull. The heat grew more and more frightful, and when he tried to wipe his forehead with the back of his hand, he realized that he no longer had hands, and that his forehead had also disappeared.

"I'm going away . . ." the Investigator managed to whisper, frightened, surprised, and disappointed.

"Obviously," the Shadow said, mocking him. "Why would that astonish you? Dying shouldn't surprise a man who isn't anyone, as the Poet once wrote. But nobody reads poetry anymore. People wipe their bums with it! Besides, I informed you that you'd be disappearing soon. I haven't been underhanded with you, I never lie, I'm not made for that. Come on, for goodness' sake, improve your final moments. Give your death agony some meaning, even if you weren't able to give your life any. Answer me—you've got no more to lose. What have I founded? Tell me, damn it! Do you want me to kneel? Apparently, that used to work in the old days."

At that point, without knowing why, the Investigator thought about lilacs and their scent. He distinctly saw the pale-purple clusters of their flowers, blooming on a May morning in a distant spring, and he breathed in their pungent, sweet perfume. Then he was on a ship—standing on its prow, to be exact—that was making more than thirty knots; he held the rail with both hands while the sea spray streamed down his face, leaving on his lips the delicious taste of water and salt, and pods of dolphins leaped out of the frothy waves, caressed by the siren song arising from the light-dazzled air. He also saw an infant emerge from its mother's womb, saw the spread thighs, heard the wail coming from the little body, successfully delivered, and watched the mother's tears mingling with the blood and matter of nascent life. He was right in the middle of a dancing crowd, celebrating the return of peace after a war that had claimed millions of victims. He whirled about, was embraced by women who pressed their warm lips to his, saw their laughter, their eyes glittering with joy, and he caressed their hips and their breasts, forgot himself in them, and then, suddenly, everything was gone.

"We could go on with more images if I let you have your way," the Shadow said, sounding piqued. "It's easy to believe in happiness. All you have to do is graft a few moments like those onto one or two of your brain cells, and the thing is done. I've offered you the opportunity of enjoying those last little pleasures that you've never known, I've given you a few false, two-bit memories, to prove to you that I'm not a bad old guy, but answer me now! I want to hear it from the mouth of a man! What am I supposed to have founded?

So what had become of that big, incandescent sun? And

that vast plain, with its chalky soil? Was it night at last? The Investigator, unable to make out anything anymore, considered those questions, helplessly aware that his meager remaining strength was leaving him.

"Not yet," the Shadow whispered to him. "Not yet. That would be too simple. The night . . . the night's for later."

And yet everything had begun so normally. In a train station similar to many other train stations. On a square much like the other such squares that exist innumerably all over the Earth. Inside a bar of the most ordinary sort. Why had everything become so complicated after that? He'd set foot in a town, or in a life. He'd crossed paths with figures, with persons who stood for millions of others. He'd tried to unconfuse the issue, to give things names, to make them simple and clear, to go where he'd been told to go, to do what he'd been told to do. In the very beginning, even the account of events had followed established codes and depended on comforting structures before starting to free itself from them, to let itself go, to saw off the branches on which it had rested for so long, to do its part in bewildering him still more.

"I had an Investigation to conduct," breathed the Investigator, trying in vain to touch his chin to his chest, which no longer existed. "An Investigation I wasn't even able to begin . . ."

"How do you know? Who says you haven't conducted a successful Investigation? You've located me, haven't you? And to hear you tell it, I'm the Founder, right?"

"I wasn't looking for you. I had an Investigation . . ." the Investigator murmured, before his lips dissolved, and with them his face.

"*By not seeking, you shall find.* Am I perhaps the cause

of all this as well as its consequence? The beginning of the loop, the end of the loop? How do you know? You call me the Founder, but who knows, I could also be the Gravedigger, couldn't I? That would suit me better! Think about all those containers! I'm surrounded by corpses. Come on, hurry up and answer my question, you're not eternal. You've asserted that you were the Investigator. You had a mission, a role, a purpose, and even if you don't think you reached your goal, the fact nevertheless remains that you know who you are and why you are who you are, but as for me, who am I, really? A broom was placed in my hands, I no longer know when, and it never made much sense anyway. What is my function? What do you think I've founded? *What am I the Founder of?*" the Shadow bellowed, and his reverberating cry set off a cascade of echoes that crashed against one another in a prolonged fall, inflicting mutual damage and making Heaven and Earth shake with dreadful thunder.

The Shadow was waiting, but the Investigator turned away from him, for he saw ghostly figures coming to greet him as in a ceremony of condolence: silhouettes, ideas, recollections, holograms, fictional characters, among whom he clearly recognized the Policeman, the Giantess, who smiled at him, the Guide, the Manager, the Server, the Security Officer and the Guard, the Child with the burning eyes, the Psychologist, who hung back a little, the Tourists, the Displacees, the Crowd. They all seemed somewhat ill at ease as they spent a few moments in silence before the body of a man of average size, with a round face and a balding pate, a man who resembled them like a brother, who was the victim of a farce in which they'd played their roles without trying very hard to step out of them, because it's more comfortable that way. They had always been well ahead of the Investigator, and so they remained, even if that didn't help them in any way and wouldn't save them.

There were still some letters, drawn by a hand writing on a blackboard. A needle piercing a vein to draw out blood or inject some liquid. A very clear image of slow dripping and the soothing music it produced, soon covered by the sound of sheets of paper being torn up and then burned, and the faint whisper of ink poured out onto the pages of a book.

"So what have I founded!!!???" the Shadow shouted for the last time.

In the Investigator's weak, doomed heart, there still trembled one or two mute words, barely formed, before what remained of his consciousness was carried off into the void, like the last puff of a cigarette in the wind. Then everything in him died, the answer to the question, the signs, the traces of light, his memory, his doubts. He thought he heard a slight noise, like the sound made by the lid of a laptop computer when the screen is closed on keys still warm from the fingertips that have caressed them so long.

"Click."

And then—nothing more.

Nothing more.

Philippe Claudel is the author of many
novels, among them *Brodeck*, which won
the Prix Goncourt des Lycéens in 2007 and
the Independent Foreign Fiction Prize in
2010. His novel *By a Slow River* has been
translated into thirty languages and was
awarded the Prix Renaudot in 2003 and
the Elle Readers' Literary Prize in 2004.
Claudel also wrote and directed the 2008
film *I've Loved You So Long*, starring
Kristin Scott Thomas, which won a BAFTA
Award for Best Film Not in the English
Language.

This book was set in a typeface called
Walbaum. The original cutting of this
face was made by Justus Erich Walbaum
(1768–1839) in Weimar in 1810. The type
was revived by the Monotype Corporation
in 1934. Young Walbaum began his artistic
career as an apprentice to a maker of cookie
molds. How he managed to leave this field
and become a successful punch cutter
remains a mystery. Although the type
that bears his name may be classified as
modern, numerous slight irregularities in
its cut give this face its humane manner.